listen to the children

listen to the children

a novel

Johnny Bloodworth

Johnny Bloodworth (signature)

Deeds Publishing | Athens

Published by Deeds Publishing in Athens, GA
www.deedspublishing.com

Printed in The United States of America

Cover design by Mark Babcock. Text layout by Matt King.

Library of Congress Cataloging-in-Publications data is available upon request.

ISBN 978-1-947309-82-1

Books are available in quantity for promotional or premium use. For information, email info@deedspublishing.com.

First Edition, 2019

10 9 8 7 6 5 4 3 2 1

To all my friends and relatives that read Gift and encouraged me to keep writing. Thanks. This is for you.

Prologue, Winnsboro Mills, SC

When it was the closing hymn, Lavinia Tuttle always sang the first verse of *Amazing Grace* solo and without Ester's wheezy organ accompaniment. Lavinia's voice was clear, and the notes were pure. When she sang "a wretch like me," most agreed she had it right. Beyond her voice, there was no beauty to Lavinia. She was straight lines and angles, sharp angles. To say she was skinny would be generous. Despite her lack of size, she had volume. Where it came from, no one knew.

The congregation joined at the second verse and mostly finished together, except for Ester's organ which held on to the last note until it suffocated. Before the benediction, Pastor Riley announced, "All children ages ten to fourteen meet with Miss Tuttle at three to start practice for the Christmas program."

He knew it was coming, still Albert Samples winced at the announcement. He knew his momma would make him go, just like she had the last two years. He liked to sing and could; his daddy and uncles could sing too. Most Saturday nights they would all go to one uncle's house or another's, eat supper, and sing. Those were good times. He didn't look forward to spending his Sunday afternoons with Miss Tuttle even though his daddy wouldn't let him play ball or do anything fun after church.

Twelve showed for the practice, five boys and seven girls. Two of the boys were in his class at school and the other two were older. Frank Hafner was there too. Albert knew he was too old. He had been the main singer for the past two years. *Maybe he's going to help. I hope not. He's a real asshole, and I can sing better than him.*

Miss Tuttle came in and she went right to Frank and talked to him. He left, and he didn't look happy about it. She looked over the group and said, "Each of you is going to sing the first verse of *Jesus Loves Me* by yourself."

After singing, he knew he was the best boy singer and only Maria Causey among the girls could sing at all. One of the older boy's voice kept going up and down and Miss Tuttle made a face, but you couldn't say it was a bad face given what she started with.

"Albert and Maria stand here," Miss Tuttle ordered. Her long skinny finger pointed to places for the rest on either side. She started with *Silent Night.* "Albert, Maria, sing louder." She put her hand on a squeaky voiced boy's shoulder, "You, don't sing, pretend."

They sang five carols twice. Miss Tuttle seemed in a hurry, and they were done by four.

Albert looked at Maria, *I'll ask her if I can walk home with her, and we can talk about our songs.*

Miss Tuttle called, "Albert."

Turning away from Maria, Albert answered, "Ma'am?"

Freddy, one of the fourteen-year-olds, said something to Maria, and Albert watched them walk out as Miss Tuttle continued,

"Albert, you have a nice voice, but it needs training. I want you to come home with me this afternoon for a special lesson. We finished early so you won't be late getting home."

Oh, shit. "Yes'm." *Why do I have to go home with this ugly woman? I'll bet Freddy will get something off Maria.*

The house was small, four rooms and a bathroom. It was dark. Curtains covered one window in the living room, and an old upright Baldwin piano blocked the other. "Go to the bathroom, Albert," Miss Tuttle directed. "I am going to change clothes."

"I don't need to."

"Go anyway, you will feel better, and we have work to do. Be sure to wash your hands and dry them well."

"Yes'm." *What the hell is going on with this crazy lady. I know when I gotta pee.* Albert flushed the toilet and walked to the living room. With no lamp on, he almost couldn't see.

"Now," Miss Tuttle said as she came into the room wearing a long dress with a tie in front. Switching on a lamp beside the piano, she sat on the bench facing him. "Stand here. Albert, you have a nice voice. No, a very good voice, but you sing from your throat. Take off your shirt down to the skin."

"Ma'am?"

"Go on. Get it off."

He tugged off his undershirt and dropped it on the floor beside his shirt. His chest and shoulders showed some coming manhood, and there was the odor.

"Albert," she said. "your lungs are here." and she placed her hands on his breasts. "Take a big breath and sing a note."

A not unpleasant "Laaaa," came from him.

She dropped her hands to below his ribs. "Take another big

breath and push out right here and hold it. When I push, sing the note again."

The note sounded a little different at first, then it sounded like the first one.

"It's a start. But let me show you." Miss Tuttle stood, untied her dress and let the sleeves fall from her arms. It fell over the bench as she sat.

She's naked! Not a thing on! What's going on? I gotta get the hell out of here. Albert couldn't move.

"Give me your hands." Not waiting, she took them, pulled him closer and placed one on each of her almost non-existent breasts. "Your hands are cold. We'll wait a moment until they warm."

Having a breast in his hand was something Albert had thought about. He had thought about it a lot. He had thought about it this afternoon when he saw Maria Causey. *Maria's titties are way bigger than Miss Tuttle's.* He closed his hands a little and Miss Tuttle moved a little and released his hands from hers.

"Good. Your hands are getting warmer."

He closed his hands more, almost squeezing. It seemed she moved toward him. He looked down as Miss Tuttle spread her legs a bit wider.

"Hold tight." she said. "I want you to feel me breathing in my lungs." She took a breath and let it out with a note, another and another. "Could you feel my breathing, Albert?"

"Yes," he answered, but he hadn't even heard the notes.

"That was throat singing like you do. Now I want you see how it feels when I sing from lower in my chest." She took his hands and moved them below her waist to the top of her open legs and released them. "Albert, you know your hands are not in the right place, don't you?"

"Yes'm." As he looked, he saw her legs open even more. Albert didn't move his hands.

"Move them up until I tell you to stop. We'll have another hand practice later." She stopped him when his hands were below her ribs. "Now you push in when I start to sing."

Her stomach moved out against his hands with the breath she took. He pushed as she sang the first note of *Amazing Grace*. Albert's ears hurt it was so loud, and she held it much longer than the church version.

"Do you hear the difference?"

"Yes'm."

"Do you want to learn to sing properly?"

"Yes'm"

"You will do as I say and not tell anyone."

"Yes'm."

"You know how that boy's voice kept going up and down?"

"Yes'm."

"His voice was changing. It is a part of growing up. Your voice will change too. Now I want to find out when your voice will change so I will know how to teach you."

"Yes'm."

"Pull down your pants and underwear."

"Ma'am?"

"You heard me. Hurry."

The excitement of what he had touched and seen still held on. "But it's...uh, uh."

"I know and I need to see."

With his pants around his ankles, Albert stood looking at Miss Tuttle sitting now with her legs wide open on the piano bench a foot from him.

"No hair yet," she said, "and not much girth." She slid her hands up and down. In less than a minute, Albert cried out and bent over. "Nothing yet," she said. "I'll make it happen soon. Turn around and bend over."

Albert complied without question. As soon as he bent, he felt an explosion of pain across his rear, and he fell sprawling to the floor. Fighting tears, he turned over and saw the naked Miss Tuttle standing astride him with a big wooden paddle in her hands.

"Albert, I can give you music, and I can give you pleasure. But I can also give you pain. Not like this paddle, but real pain. Don't you ever cross me, or don't you ever tell. Now get dressed and come tomorrow after school for your next lesson." She closed her gown and walked out of the room.

Albert dressed quickly and ran home.

The next day, Miss Tuttle made him practice singing for two hours. Not songs, but notes, and not singing from his throat. She showed him how to hold his hand over his ear to hear his voice better. Nothing else happened, and he walked home in the dark. With one hand over his ear and the other pushing his stomach he sang the notes of the scale. Albert liked the way he sounded.

The next practice was Sunday afternoon. The boy Miss Tuttle told to pretend to sing didn't come back, and Freddy and Maria came in together. Albert thought they all sounded better this week, but only because he thought he was better. They finished quicker than he expected, and Miss Tuttle told him to come home with her for more practice. There were lessons, but no singing and no paddles.

The Christmas program went well. Pastor Riley thanked Miss Tuttle and said how blessed they were to have her as a member of their congregation. A few of the older girls came over to Albert and told him they liked his singing. When Miss Tuttle came over the girls drifted away. She told Albert to come for a lesson. This time Miss Tuttle got what she liked. Albert knew what happened, and he thought well of himself. It changed some of their activities until Miss Tuttle could get to a drug store in Columbia.

II — 1938

Albert's voice started changing in the early spring. He was a tenor, but now there was a depth and richness which hadn't been there before. It seemed Miss Tuttle worked more on his voice during the summer, and by the time school started it had settled down. She told him he was a good singer now but would get better. "We are going to sing a duet at the end of October, *How Great Thou Art*."

Next to *Amazing Grace*, *How Great Thou Art* was Miss Tuttle's other song. She always sang it all as a solo and never with any accompaniment.

"I'm going to ask Dorothy from the Methodist Church if she will play the piano with us. Our organ is not right for what I want to do. I am going to sing the verses, and you and I will harmonize on the refrain. Dorothy will play very quietly except, I will let her take a verse in the middle."

Miss Tuttle hit the first note of the refrain for pitch and moved her hand for tempo. Albert kept his hand over his ear and tried to find the place to match Miss Tuttle's soprano. *Damn, we sound pretty good. Miss Ester is not going to be happy about not playing for this. I could do a verse.*

"Albert, pay attention."

The performance went well. Pastor Riley had tears in his eyes when it ended and said he really didn't need to preach. But he did anyway, and for forty-five minutes. At the end, he announced the ten to fourteen-year-olds should meet with Miss Tuttle to prepare for the Christmas program.

This year, Albert was the oldest. Maria and Freddy and the other boy were gone, and they didn't have but ten. One was a new kid who had moved to town when school started. He was in seventh grade and could sing a little. The only girl who could sing much was Helen Jones. She was twelve and kind of heavy. When they all finished *Jesus Loves Me*, Miss Tuttle put Albert and Helen in front and the new kid beside Helen. They finished quickly and Albert asked about a lesson. Miss Tuttle told him "Not this afternoon, come on Wednesday." Albert saw her talk to Henry, the new kid.

On Wednesday, Miss Tuttle told Albert their lessons were over. "I've taught you all I can about singing. It is time for you to learn more on your own. Besides, you have grown up."

"What about the other things we did?"

"With us, it is all over."

"But I liked it."

"We are over Albert, unless you tell. Remember what I told you about real pain, besides no one would believe you. They wouldn't listen to children's talk about this. Oh yes, you will do the Christmas program. Maybe you can help one of the girls with their singing. Now, go."

Albert was angry. *What the hell could she do if I told? Her paddle didn't hurt that bad. Hell, my dad's beatings are way worser. What would I tell? She played with my peter and let me touch her everywhere. Let me? She made me. And we even screwed. She's right, they wouldn't listen.*

When he got home, he went into the bedroom he shared with his brothers and sat on the bed. He called to his mother saying he didn't want any supper. Albert sat until he finally fell asleep.

The next Sunday at program practice, he tried to sing badly, but he couldn't. He liked to hear his new voice. He decided to sing better, better than he ever had. When practice was over, early as he suspected, Miss Tuttle left quickly with Henry. He was left there with Helen Jones and skinny little Lillian Gish Poovey.

"Helen, you have a nice voice." Albert said. "But you sing too much from your throat. Would you like me to teach you to sing better?"

"Yes, I would, Albert. What should I do?" Helen replied.

"I would like to learn too." said Lillian Gish.

"I can only teach one at a time. Let me and Helen have a lesson and after maybe I'll teach you." *At least Helen's got some titties.*

"Can we start now?" asked Helen.

"Yes, right here. Lillian wait outside."

It only took a minute to figure out Helen wasn't going to take off her shirt for singing or for him. But she could sing a little.

After a few minutes, he asked her to wait outside and to tell Lillian to come in. Her first notes were sort of screeches, but he actually heard something in her voice he liked. She didn't bat an eye when he took off his shirt and put her hands on his breasts and on his stomach. And, she didn't hesitate at all when he asked her to take off her shirt. Lillian Gish had six brothers, four older and two younger. Being bare chested in front of a boy was nothing to her, naked didn't bother her either.

All of her older brothers had taken turns at her, and she at her younger brothers. It was the way it was. So, when Albert asked her to pull down her panties so he could check to see when her voice would change, she looked at him and said, "You first."

"Okay. But my voice has already changed. You can tell. After I do, you'll have to." And he pulled his pants and underwear down. Lillian smiled and reached out and wrapped her hand around him.

Giggling, she said, "You sure do have a skinny peter. My eight-year-old brother's is bigger than yours. Yours looks like a pink color crayon except you've got some hair." She gave it a little twist and hooked her thumbs in the waist of her skirt and pulled skirt and underpants down in one move. Thrusting forward she asked "What do you think? Pretty nice, huh? And, I'm getting some titties. See." She took his hand and placed it over one swollen nipple. "Now," as she took hold again, "What do you want me to do with this little crayon of yours?"

He jerked his hand away from her nipple and screamed "You lint-head Poovey bitch!" He took a wild swing at her. Still holding on, Lillian pulled her head back, and he missed badly. She wanted to kick him, but with her skirt and underpants around her ankles she couldn't. So, she moved her hand to his balls, tightened her hold and squeezed as hard as she could.

Albert tried to twist away, but Lillian didn't let go. The pain kicked in. He made a gagging sound and bent forward from the waist. His knees gave way and he fell to the Sunday School room floor. Lillian released her grip as he fell. She looked at him for a moment, pulled up her underpants and skirt, buttoned her shirt and put on her jacket.

Albert was on the floor with his pants still around his ankles and his shirt laying on a chair. He was hardly moving, and his hands were clamped over his injury.

At the door, Lillian looked as he rolled over toward her. "To hell with you and your pink color crayon peter," she said, and she stuck up her middle finger and walked out.

Helen was not in the hall. Lillian called when she got outside.

Almost in a whisper "Are you okay?" came from behind a bush. Helen stepped out. "I heard him holler a bad word, and I tried to find Pastor Riley or somebody. I was scared."

"I'm fine. We can go home now. We don't need Pastor Riley."

The two oldest of Lillian Gish's four brothers had already moved out. After supper she told Roscoe, her brother who was a year older than Albert, what had happened. Roscoe didn't mind the part about Albert getting her to pull her panties down, or even trying to hit her. He laughed hard at her description of Albert and what she did. What set him off was Albert calling her a "lint-head". He said it was an insult to the family. "Ain't no goddamn Samples trash gonna talk about us that-a-way."

The next day after school, Roscoe caught Albert. He pushed

him behind the vacant house next door and beat hell out of him. Roscoe punched Albert in the body so his face wouldn't show the beating. For the second day in a row, a Poovey left a nearly unconscious Albert with a parting "to hell with you."

Albert got into his room without being seen by his mother. He called to her to say he didn't feel well and didn't want any supper. He never undressed and covered his head. He slept fitfully for a while in the bed he shared with his younger brother. About eleven o'clock he got his jacket and slipped out of the house.

He stayed on the other side of the street when he walked past Lavinia Tuttle's house. There were no lights on. At the corner, he turned and eased down the alley to her backyard. The key was under the next to last flower pot on the right. From the kitchen, he could hear her snore, not loudly, but a gentle lady's snore.

Standing beside her bed he heard the voice of Lillian Gish Poovey, "pink color crayon peter." Albert took the brass lamp on the bedside table and crashed it into the sleeping Lavinia's face as hard as he could. He hit her twice more and looked. Against the white pillow was a dark spot where her face had been. Her snoring was replaced by a gurgling as air bubbled through blood in her throat.

Albert pulled the bedclothes down to the bottom of the bed. *She has on the white gown. It won't be white long.* He pushed the front of the gown to her shoulders and over her bloody face and pressed it down. A wet moan came from Lavinia. He spread her legs and heard another weak sound. "I hope you hurt," he said.

He took off his pants and crawled on the bed. Two minutes later, he was done. In the kitchen, he found a big knife and stabbed her hard through each breast. With the second thrust, he could feel the blade of the knife bounce off bone as it plunged deeper. He added a third wound where she had him touch her when she showed him how to breathe. Lavinia stopped making sounds after the first knife wound.

At the foot of the bed, he smiled then panicked. Fingerprints! What did I touch? A quick, but incomplete, list came to him—the lamp, the knife, the key, doorknobs. With a towel from the bathroom, he wiped things on his list working his way to the kitchen. He wiped the knife and put it in the drawer then pushed the drawer closed. He held the towel over the knob when he opened the door and locked it from outside.

In the alley, he stuffed the towel in a garbage can and threw up. At the street, he dropped the key in a drain. Walking home, he avoided every street light and car. It was after one o'clock when he slipped into bed with his little brother.

The next day after recess, his teacher gave the class some old spelling words to copy and went out into the hall. Copying old spelling words meant something was going on, and the teacher wanted to get out of the room. Albert guessed they found Miss Tuttle. He was right.

Two days later, Charlie Baker found the body of Lillian Gish Poovey at the back of his lot. She was still warm, and blood oozed from her nose and one ear. Her dress was around her waist and her underwear was down to her feet. A chunk of granite the size of a softball lay beside her caved-in skull. Charlie ran a block to Robert White's house, and told him what he found, and to call Sheriff Kitt. He returned to the body and noticed something he had not seen when he first found her. The end of a pink, round school crayon was sticking from her vagina. He had to walk away. When Robert White came, he could only stand a quick look at Lillian Gish's body.

Sheriff Kitt came with the night deputy. Shortly after, two of the detectives from Columbia who had come to investigate Miss Tuttle's murder arrived at Baker's house.

Sheriff Kitt pulled Baker and White aside. He said, "Keep quiet about the crayon. I don't want anybody to know about it. It might be what gives the killer away."

Charlie looked at the sheriff, "Lewis, I don't think I could ever tell what I saw here." Charlie's silence lasted three days, one day after the funeral.

Like the news of Miss Tuttle's murder, the word got to the school at recess. It went through the teachers in a few minutes, and then it started down through the grades. Somebody told Roscoe about the pink crayon, and he screamed, "I'll kill him. I'll kill the son of a bitch."

Albert heard him.

The next morning, the milkman found Roscoe's body in front of the vacant house next to the Samples' house.

In his statement, Sheriff Kitt said, "The child had been shot in the back of the head with what looked like a .22 rifle. His shirt was ripped open, and he had been stabbed in each breast and in his belly below his ribs." He didn't say the knife was still in the belly wound when they found him. Or, Roscoe's mother said the knife had come from their house.

The sheriff had called Columbia for help when they found Miss Tuttle's body. Some of the state detectives were in town when Lillian Gish's body was found. They, and more, came when

Roscoe was killed. Their word was the same person did all three killings. They had fingerprints, but no real suspects. It seemed like they talked to and fingerprinted every unmarried man, white or colored, in the area. They added the drinkers. Two or three got locked up for a day or two. No one ever talked to Albert.

III — 1942

With the start of the war, church attendance was better. Albert tried to sing in the adult choir. The new choir leader was a retired constable from Columbia, but he didn't know anything about singing. He yelled a lot, and Albert quit after a month.

One Saturday evening when the family was all together, his uncle said, "Albert, when you pay attention you are about as good a singer as I know."

"Thanks, Uncle Bob. I like to sing."

"There's going to be an amateur night down at the Township in Columbia in three weeks. How about we work up a tune and try out? I've been working on *My Blue Heaven*."

Saturday night they took third place, made two dollars, and got into the semi-finals. From the second he and Uncle Bob walked out onto the big stage, Albert knew he had to perform and be in front of people. If he wasn't performing or practicing, his thoughts returned to the other things Lavinia Tuttle taught him. For them, he was on his own. After Lillian Gish Poovey, he knew he would never have a girlfriend.

The next year he was a senior. Albert, a cousin, and Malcolm Ledwell formed a trio, two guitars and Albert singing. They played a few places. The two on guitars could get close to most any tune, and Albert would make the song work. They made a little money and had fun. It seemed to others, the two always had girls waiting for them after they played.

Malcolm's daddy sold timber, made money, ran around, and drank. A Thursday evening in early April, he listened to them practice for a few minutes. "Damn, you boys are pretty good." He stepped closer and motioned them to him. "With all this young poon' that's flocking around y'all at these clubs, you need some experience."

"Daddy," an embarrassed Malcolm said.

"Hush, boy. I'm going to do something for you my daddy did for me. Over past Ridgeway, out toward the river on Longtown Road, there's a place. I know you've heard of it and know where it is. Anyway, the girls are looking for you tonight. It's all paid, but you might take your guitars, play 'em a tune and get a little extra."

Malcom's father was right. Every high school boy in the county knew the place by reputation, but none had ever come close to going in.

Albert's cousin, Bruce, nudged him with an elbow and smiled. Albert didn't react.

"Son," Malcolm's daddy said, "take the old pickup. I don't want nobody to see our car over there. There's a jar of courage in a poke on the floor. You might learn a little about it too."

The jar of courage lasted Bruce and Malcolm as far as Ridgeway. As soon as they got through town, Malcolm had to pull over for Bruce to puke.

Though none of them or their friends had ever dared to make the turn into the lane, they all knew it. No house was visible from the road, but after a turn, there was a light. It was a neat little house with a light beside the front door. Bruce knocked.

"Come in, boys. We've been expecting you." The speaker had yellow blonde hair, big red lips, and drawn on eyebrows that nearly disappeared into her hair. "My girls are in the parlor."

"She's old," Bruce whispered too loudly.

"Quiet, Bruce," Albert said. "You're drunk."

As they entered the parlor, two women in long dressing gowns smiled from chairs on either side of a small table. One stood.

"I'm Amanda," she said, "and this is Deborah. We are glad to see you this evening."

Deborah said, "Oh, good, you brought your instruments. You'll play for us, won't you?"

The yellow haired lady said, "I'm Miss Dixie. There is tea and lemonade on the table. Please, help yourself."

Again, too loudly, Bruce said, "They ain't girls. They're old too." And in a more normal voice, "I need something to drink. The lemonade sounds good."

Miss Dixie pointed to a chair and said, "Have a seat there, and I will fix your lemonade. Amanda, Deborah, go ahead and take the boys back."

Albert went into the small dimly lit bedroom with Deborah. "Put your clothes on the chair," she said as she sat on the edge of the bed. With his back to her, Albert slipped his shorts off and turned. "Socks, too," she said as she stood.

Naked Albert was standing face to face with Deborah. She

smiled, untied the gown and opened it. In a practiced move she tossed it to the foot of the bed.

Deborah was everything in a woman Lavinia Tuttle was not. Albert swallowed hard. Since Lavinia and Lillian Gish, Albert had forced the thoughts and feeling he was having now out of his head. But, now three years of hormones and passion came rushing back. He put his hands on her breasts and squeezed.

"Easy," Deborah said.

Albert mumbled, "Sorry. Get on the bed."

"Yes, sir," Deborah said mockingly as she sat and lay back on the bed.

Albert ignored her tone and climbed on after, kneeling at the foot. He spread her legs wide apart and looked.

In a moment, Deborah said, "Are you ready?"

Albert nodded and crawled forward.

"Done already?" Deborah asked. "Get dressed and go have some tea."

In the parlor, Miss Dixie gave him tea though he hadn't asked. In a few minutes, Malcolm came from the other room. He was smiling. Miss Dixie fixed Malcolm tea and went into Amanda's room.

Malcolm said, "She said I was good, a stud, and she ought to know." He took his guitar. "If we play, we might get seconds." He strummed the opening chords of *My Blue Heaven*, but Albert didn't attempt to sing. "Sing, Albert. Go on and sing."

"Yes, sing for us, Albert," Miss Dixie said as she and Amanda returned to the parlor.

Amanda sat beside Albert on the small couch and put her hand on his shoulder. "Was that *My Blue Heaven*? Please sing."

Malcolm tapped his guitar and played a short introduction. Albert started singing. He lost himself in the music. Miss Dixie sat, and Amanda leaned back on the couch and closed her eyes. Malcolm eased into *Love Walked In* and Albert followed. Bruce picked up his guitar when he came from Deborah's room. They played for another twenty minutes, mostly quiet ballads. Amanda and Deborah danced to one tune and seemed to hold each other very close. Miss Dixie made a little noise and looked at them, and they sat down.

"Girls," Miss Dixie said, "Don't you think these boys have earned a special treat?"

Amanda and Deborah smiled and walked to their respective doors. Malcolm stood and walked to Deborah. Amanda motioned to Bruce who was standing, and they entered her room.

"Albert," Miss Dixie said, "You really do have a lovely voice. Have you ever had lessons?"

"Not really," he answered.

"You do sing well. Now," she continued, "You boys can come any time you like, except Sundays and Mondays. For one time with one of my girls, it is four dollars. If you come on Tuesday or Wednesday, it is half price and it is not so crowded. You be sure and tell the others."

Malcolm came from Deborah's room.

"You want to wait for Amanda, don't you, Albert?" Miss Dixie asked.

"No, ma'am."

"Well then, wait a minute," and Miss Dixie walked into Deborah's room.

Alone in the parlor, Malcolm said, "You ain't going to believe what she did to me. It was amazing. And, we did the regular too. Tell her you want what I got. Tell her, Albert."

Miss Dixie stood at the door and motioned for Albert.

Albert quickly got what he wanted and nothing more.

As he was pulling on his pants, Deborah said, "You sure do sing pretty, Little Man. Come back any time and ask for me."

Little man, little man—Albert said nothing.

On the ride home, Malcolm and Bruce told and retold every detail of their adventure. Albert drove and paid them no mind.

Every time he could scrape together two dollars, and get a car to drive, he made the trip to Miss Dixie's. If he was inside more than fifteen minutes, it was only because Deborah had another customer. A few times, Miss Dixie said Deborah wasn't available and he left.

Albert, Bruce, and Malcolm were among the thirty who graduated from the Mount Zion Institute on Thursday, June 6, 1943. On Friday, they and most of the other boys in the class enlisted. All were to report to Camp Jackson, outside of Columbia, on the following Wednesday.

After supper on Tuesday, he took Malcolm's dad's pickup truck and drove to Miss Dixie's. It was nearly dark when he arrived.

"Good, you are by yourself," Miss Dixie said as she opened the door. "Amanda's in Columbia tonight. Deborah, you have a caller."

"So, my little man's going to be a soldier," Deborah said. "We'll have to do something special."

"Yeah, maybe," Albert said.

When Albert finished, he stood and took his pants from the

chair. Uncovered and nude and lying spread out in the bed, Deborah asked, "Nothing special, Little Man?"

"Turn over," Albert said and let his pants fall.

As she turned, Deborah said, "I guess you'll have something to tell the other recruits about."

"Not likely," he said as he opened the blade on his Barlow knife, grabbed Deborah's hair, reached around and slit her throat. She flailed with her arms, but he never loosened his hold on her hair. He could see her mouth moving, but no sounds came out. Albert let go and Deborah's face fell into the growing blood spot on her bed.

Still nude himself, Albert cracked the door open and called to Miss Dixie, "Ma'am…, Miss Dixie, come in here. Something is wrong with Deborah.

Dixie came in and stopped at the foot of the bed. Albert grabbed her by the hair, but her yellow wig came off in his hand. Miss Dixie started for the door, and Albert lunged after her. He could feel his knife hit the side of her neck. He pushed it as deep as he could and twisted it. Her knees buckled. Albert let her go, and she fell to the floor splattering blood as her failing heart pumped it out of the gash in her neck.

Albert felt something warm on his bare knee. He looked down to see a big drop of Miss Dixie's blood start to run down his leg. "Damn!" He stepped to Miss Dixie's body and wiped his knee clean with the hem of her dress. He didn't notice he stepped on another spot of blood on the floor. His next two steps on the dark wooden floor left heel prints. He took his clothes to the parlor, dressed and left. At the first creek he crossed, he stopped and threw in the Barlow knife.

Deputy Wilkes stood outside the door to the sheriff's office smoking. He watched as a pickup truck turned into the drive and skidded to a stop.

"Where's the sheriff?" Charlie Moore hollered.

"Hell, Charlie, it's ten o'clock at night. I 'spect he's home." He flicked his cigarette on the ground and stepped on it. "What's got you in such a state?"

"There's been a killin' out at Miss Dixie's. Her and one of her girls, throats cut and a lot of blood."

"I'll call him," the deputy said. When he returned, he had a camera and a shoulder bag. "Sheriff Kitt says for you to follow me out to Miss Dixie's. I'm going to get him right now."

"Shit, Frank. I can't go out there. If Miss Willie even thought I knew where the place was, you'd have another killing. Tell Lewis, I'd gone when you came out. He'll understand."

Sheriff Kitt found the heel prints, but they were the only things that looked like evidence. Frank took pictures. Thursday, an agent from the state lifted the heel print and fingerprints.

Wednesday morning, Albert, six others and their families met at the clock to wait for the bus to take the recruits to Camp Jackson. The bus had started in Lancaster and stopped in Great Falls. By the time it got to Winnsboro, it was half full.

The driver opened the door and stepped out, "Get on board, boys. No luggage. If you need it, the Army will give it to you. Double time, boys, I've got two more in Blythewood, and you are in the Army." The bus started five minutes after it stopped. Seven crying mommas waved as the bus headed south on Congress Street.

IV—1943

Albert survived basic training and the June heat at Camp Jackson. He was assigned to the artillery school at Fort Sill, Oklahoma. The next cycle of school didn't begin for ten days. KP and other busy work took care of his days, nights he spent at the USO. A small dance band played most nights, and he talked the leader into letting him sing a number or two. The leader and the crowd liked him, and by the second weekend, he was a regular. When his training started, he still was able to sing. A colonel from Special Services heard him. Two weeks later, Albert Samples was transferred. He spent the duration as a performer, director, and producer of shows for soldiers and sailors all over the Pacific Theater. Albert loved his job and was very good at it.

1945

Standing in the open door and speaking inside, the corporal said, "Sargent Crosby, there will be a car to take you to the airfield at 1400."

Albert waited as the corporal started to close the door. "Oh," he said as he turned. "Afternoon, Sargent. Looks like you are going to have a private room for a while."

"Bill, what's going on? Are you leaving?" Albert asked the man stuffing the last of his gear into a duffle bag.

"I'm going to the States. I will be on Armed Forces Radio. I don't know exactly what I will do, but you may soon hear these dulcet tones anywhere in the world."

"Gee, really tough duty."

"Yeah, somebody's got to do it, and it might work out for something after this war's over. Albert, what are you going to do after? Show business, New York, Hollywood? You are good at putting shows together, and you can sing."

"Maybe, but you don't have to be in the big time to make a little money with a show. The summer after tenth grade, I went around with a tent preacher."

"Tent preaching ain't show business," Bill said.

"Yes, hell it is. Every week was a three-act play. He'd find him a shill, me for most of the summer. I'd be the sinner. Brother Stephen, that's what he liked to be called, would damn me on Thursday. He could scare you bad with his description of hell. Friday, I'd repent, crying, carrying on and all. Usually I'd sing *Amazing Grace*. Hell, half the tent would come to the altar confessing sins and leaving change on the rail. I'd be redeemed on Saturday. I'd testify and call the congregation to the altar."

He had it all scripted out. He'd change who he saved and why each week. There was a girl who came around every few weeks and played a fallen woman. That weren't no stretch for her, and she could make you cry."

"He didn't make any money, did he?"

"He could have. Me and the colored organ player worked out an arrangement of *Just as I Am* that would bring a heathen like you to your knees. You'd open your wallet too. Those lint-heads and dirt farmers sure did."

"What happened?"

"Mostly he drank the profits. He was no good with the music either, that's why he liked me. Between the whiskey and widows, not much money stuck." Albert paused, "Brother Stephen always thought of himself as a martyr, and I guess he was. Bill, I was fixing to go down to the Surf Club. Join me and I'll pay—a going away present."

"Ain't got time. I'm not quick like you, and besides, I want my money's worth, or even your money's worth. But Albert, why do you always go to whore houses? With all those girls in your shows, and the ones that hang around when you sing, you wouldn't have to pay for anything but a drink."

"Girls, real girls are too much trouble. Besides, I don't have time for any of the other stuff that goes along with girlfriends. I'm okay with pay as you go at the Surf Club."

Bill reached in his pocket and pulled out a small medicine bottle. "Maybe you could use some of this."

"What?"

"Knock out drops," Bill answered. "Two drops in a drink makes a Mickey Finn cocktail. Give your girl one, she's out, or nearly out, and you're done before she wakes up. And, mostly she doesn't remember. If they do, sometimes you can even convince them the whole thing was their idea."

"Where'd you get them?"

"It's a prescription for me—to help me sleep."

"Hell, I've never seen you have trouble sleeping."

"I don't. The doc got another story."

"An Army doc gave you those?"

"Oh, hell no. I go to a civilian, a Chinaman over near Pearl. But there are plenty who will prescribe them."

"What do you do?"

Bill unscrewed the top and lifted it. There was a thin glass rod attached. As he held the rod over the open bottle two drops of clear liquid fell from the rod into the bottle. "Those two drops in a drink is usually all it takes. Whiskey or wine works best, but it will even work in a Coke. If they are small, one drop might be enough. Too much and they might not wake up."

"I don't know," Albert said.

"There's only four or five doses left in this bottle. I'll leave it for you. I have another full one in my kit. I've got a little whiskey left in a bottle. I don't need to take it with me. Since I've screwed your plan for the Surf Club, let's have a farewell drink."

"Might as well," Albert answered.

Bill found the bottle in his pack and took the two dirty glasses from the nightstand. "I'll rinse these," he said. He returned with a scant inch of whiskey in each glass and gave one to Albert. "To Armed Forces Radio and Special Services," he said and held out his glass to Albert. They touched glasses and each had a sip. "What's next for you, Albert?"

After another swallow, Albert said, "I've put together a small show. I'm going to take it to Australia." And he lay back on his cot.

Albert realized he was waking, but it was hard. *A nap? No. And, why am I laying across my cot? Maybe, I'll go back to sleep.* "Uh, uh," he moaned. He pushed to his elbows, and saw the room swirl as he opened and closed his eyes. *My knees hurt. Hell, I don't have on my pants.* He knelt and rubbed his eyes.

"Works pretty good."

"What?" Albert asked.

Bill repeated, "Works pretty good—the knock out drops."

My butt hurts, and Albert put his hands on his bare ass.

Thoughts fell into place. He said, "You gave me drops in the whiskey? You son of a bitch. I'll whip your ass."

"That's not what you said a few minutes ago."

His head cleared a little. Albert said, "You faggot, you dirty faggot, you cornholed me."

"It is war time, Al. We take what we can. And, hey, I've seen the way you look at some of those native boys. Anyway, I'm leaving you the drops. See ya." Bill grabbed his bag and left as Albert worked his way to a sitting position on the cot.

He looked at the small medicine bottle and read, *Chloral Hydrate.*

1

FRIDAY, NOVEMBER 22, 1946

"Betty May, Are we orphans?"

Elizabeth May DuBose looked across the front seat of the Packard to her little sister tucked in the corner. There was still enough light to make out the features of her ten-year-old face. She looked worried. "Connie, why did you ask?"

"Somebody called us orphans."

"When? Was it Bill's mother?"

"No, it was a little while ago."

"A little while ago? We haven't been out of the car since we left Sandy Springs. So, it was before we left?"

"No. It was while we were riding. I don't know who said it, but I heard them."

Elizabeth knew Connie's gifts. Revelations like this coming from Connie were not unusual, and they were more often right than not.

"He wants our house and our money too. I don't like it Betty May, I'm scared. Everything is so different now."

"Yes, it is, and I'm a little scared too. We have each other, and we have Bill." *Three weeks ago, I didn't know Bill Brown existed.*

Now we are engaged. "When we get home, I want you to tell me everything you felt and heard."

"Okay, but they aren't talking about us now."

Elizabeth closed her eyes for an instant as the car bumped onto the dirt of Godfrey's Store Road. They were close to home. The events of the past year went through her mind. Her daddy, Jefferson Davis DuBose, died of a heart attack in the spring. She was in her second year at GSCW, and she and her father had made plans for her to go to the University of Georgia in the fall. Those plans died with him. She came home to take care of her thirty-eight-year-old mother and her ten-year-old sister. "I'm only nineteen," she choked on the words never spoken.

"Betty May?"

"I'm okay. I'm thinking about Momma." *Momma who could talk to the spirits of the dead but couldn't or wouldn't talk to anyone else unless she had to. Momma who never thought about money or having to pay for things.*

"Momma?"

"Yes, Momma. She left us a lot to take care of."

"I'll help."

"I know. And, I need your help." *Momma was killed a week ago tomorrow in New York City, shot through the heart, by someone who knew her. Why? We buried her two days ago.*

Elizabeth turned the Packard into the lane to their house. As the car's lights lit the base of the big oak at the turn, she thought about Bill and smiled.

Connie never saw the smile, but answered it saying, "Bill will help too."

"Yes," she said, "Bill will help too." *But how? Engaged, in love, are we? We hardly know each other, and he's gone, recalled to active duty in the Army. At least he is going to be in the States. I don't know what he can do.*

Earlier the same afternoon, Hiram Tilley, the Greene County Clerk, entered the Harwell Bank. Bobby was the only teller working, and there were three in line at his barred window. Hiram walked to Bobby's window and stood beside Bill Plunkett as Bobby counted money into Bill's hand. Interrupting, "Bobby, I need to see John. Tell him I'm here."

Bobby finished his count. "Thirty-five, forty. Will there be anything else, Bill," he said to his customer.

"Not now, Bobby. I'll come later to see Mr. Harwell," Bill said as he turned toward Hiram. "Tilley," he said curtly and walked out.

"Mr. Tilley, I'll tell Mr. Harwell you're here," Bobby said. Looking to the next in line, "A second please, Mr. Howell. I'll be right with you." Bobby closed and locked his cash drawer and walked to Harwell's office. He returned quickly and said, "Please go back, Mr. Tilley."

Hiram asked, "Do you know anything more about de Graffinreed's death?"

"Yes. Hans' brother-in-law talked to a doctor at Grady. The doctor said the wound in his forehead looked like a gunshot that didn't penetrate his skull. He said it could have been a small bullet like a .22. If it had enough force it could have caused the clot. The clot caused the stroke that killed him."

"Damn, and, Mary Greene DuBose was shot too," Hiram said. "The hospital in New York sent Fred the carbon copy of the death certificate. I've got it now. It said she died from a gunshot wound that ruptured her aorta. They removed a bullet which appeared to be a .32. Hans always carried a little .32 revolver. I could believe Mary Greene would carry a little pocket gun. Hell, I think they shot each other in New York City."

"Hiram, before he went to New York, Hans told me would kill her if she didn't tell him where Jefferson hid our money. I told him, we'd never find our money if he killed her."

"What did Hans say to that?"

"He said, it's in the house, and with the conjure woman, witch or whatever you want to call her gone, we could take the house apart."

"How about the girls, John?"

"I asked him about the girls, and he said they didn't matter because they were minors. Since you were the clerk, you could appoint me to handle the estate, and we would have all the time we needed to find our money. What about it? You can't appoint me, can you?"

"No, we need a probate judge. Since Mel retired and moved, we don't have one. Judge Morrow over in Crawfordville is our acting Probate Judge."

"Would he appoint me? With me as executor and Mary dead, I might be able to solve another little problem."

"What other problem?"

"It's nothing about our business, and it's old. Forget I said anything."

"If I recommended you, I don't know why he wouldn't appoint you. Elizabeth won't be twenty-one until March of '48, and I don't know of any relatives on either side. You are a responsible, upstanding citizen with knowledge and concern for the girls and the family's affairs. I think you are the perfect choice."

"Hiram, you say Elizabeth won't be a problem, but she's pretty smart. She's run things since her daddy died last spring—signs her mother's name to everything. "

"John, she is an unmarried woman under twenty-one. Under the law, those children are orphans. Legally, she can't do diddlely. Jefferson DuBose didn't have a will, and her mother won't either. You can't take a check signed by a dead woman, right?"

"Yeah, usually that's right. But with Mary DuBose, who is to say she can't still sign a check."

"Seriously, John. Is there any money in the bank?"

"Not much, maybe a thousand dollars, enough to run the house for six or eight months. And, there's Jeff's Railroad Retirement. The check comes to Mary so all that will need to be sorted out before the girls can have any of it.

"You will have to let them have money to live on. Judge Morrow would expect that, especially since you know they are going to get the Railroad money. We will have to find out about their New York money. That is part of the estate you will have to look after. Do you have any idea about how much is in New York?"

"Not really. I know early in the war, we sold a good bit to the government, and Jefferson divvied up, but he never put any of it in my bank. I think it went straight to his New York bankers. Before Mary and the girls left for New York last week, Elizabeth told Bobby she was going to talk to her daddy's broker."

"How about debt? Do you know if Mary owed anyone?"

"I don't know of anything. There were no regular payments to anybody. I guess they owe Fred for the funeral."

"If they need money for the funeral, let her have it. Judge Morrow would appreciate your helping with the funeral."

"Yeah, so would Fred."

Hiram stood, "The tax bills were mailed yesterday. I've got it fixed where I can go to Elizabeth and rattle her a little about paying the taxes."

"There's money to pay them in the account."

"I know, John. I want her to worry some, then see me as her friend, somebody who can help with the financial things she doesn't understand."

"Hiram, you're the kind of friend every young girl needs."

"I do my best. I don't see any reason to do anything today or even next week with Thanksgiving and all. We've got to go to Martha's brothers over in Athens for the holiday. Friday I'm going bird hunting. I won't push anything until you get appointed. After I can get in to evaluate the house for the estate, we can work on the New York money. Jeff was smart. He may have found a way to get some of what we are looking for into New York banks."

"Hiram, what about de Graffinreed's family?"

"Hell, he's dead. As far as I'm concerned, they are out of it. It ain't like we had a formal agreement. I don't think his wife knew about the missing boxcar and what was in it. She knows Hans was pissed about money all the time, and he bad mouthed Jeff. I doubt she ever saw any of what Hans got. No, I think we ought to let that lie. Since the bank didn't offer me coffee, I'm going by Hunter's and get a Coke before I go to the office."

"My bank don't give nothing away, Hiram. See you later."

2

Jefferson Davis DuBose joined the Army in 1915, two days after his seventeenth birthday. After basic training, he was shipped to England and assigned to a British battalion building a light rail line to move munitions to the Channel. For the rest of the war, he worked trains and railroads. When he mustered out, he returned to Georgia and went to work for the Georgia Railroad and Banking Company. His first job was in Greensboro as the assistant depot agent. A month after he arrived in Greensboro, the depot agent dropped dead of a heart attack, DuBose took over.

In the early twenties, the Florida land boom heated up, investors began speculating on commodities, especially building materials and supplies for south Florida. Much was shipped to Florida by rail, sometimes only to a general destination. Soon rail car loads of material were stranded, and sidings well into Georgia were packed with loaded cars. Empty cars for new cargo were at a premium, and rail traffic was hindered by the blocked sidings.

DuBose had the idea of unloading the cars and sending them north. Their cargo would be stored until the sender could claim it and pay for the loading and storage. If they couldn't or wouldn't pay, he would sell the material. To make this all work, he brought in banker

John Harwell to finance the unloading, County Clerk Hiram Tilley who knew where the vacant buildings and barns were, and the depot agent from Crawfordville, Hans de Graffinreed, to help with moving the cars.

The railroads were pleased because they were getting the sidings cleared and empty cars. Georgia Railroad and Banking didn't interfere with their depot agents' side enterprise. The group only broke even through the twenties. By 1926, they had all the cars unloaded and the contents stored. After the crash and through much of the thirties, nothing sold and nothing moved. Jefferson DuBose did take a Sears and Roebuck kit house for himself and built it on a pretty hill on Godfrey's Store Road. The group gave a smaller kit house to the new sheriff, figuring it was a good investment.

As the war in Europe grew, they begin to be able to sell building materials, much to the Army. In December 1942, Jefferson told his partners all the material they stored had been sold, stolen, or rotted, and they should dissolve their business. De Graffinreed claimed there was one rail car not counted. He claimed it contained a bank safe filled with money. DuBose and de Graffinreed argued and nearly came to blows. In the end, DuBose walked away. Over the years, de Graffinreed never gave up and finally convinced Harwell and Tilley that DuBose had the safe and money hidden at his home.

Elizabeth parked the car in the shed, and they walked into the house. In the kitchen she pulled the light string. Instead of a burst of brightness, tonight it seemed like light flowed into the corners of the room and slowly filled it with a warm yellow glow. Elizabeth and Connie stood in the center of the room as their eyes went from the big refrigerator that came from a rail car, to the sink under the window with the washed and dried breakfast dishes in the rack, to the porcelain top table with the yellow legs. Elizabeth put her arm around her little sister's shoulder and pulled her close, and they both breathed out. This was familiar, this was theirs.

Connie said, "I've got to pee," and ran to the stairs. In the quiet of the house, Elizabeth heard her hit every step, turn on every light, and slam the bathroom door. They were home.

In the refrigerator, most of a baked ham was left over from the funeral food. Elizabeth cut some thin slices and piled them on halves of the morning's biscuits and put them in the oven to toast with a little grated cheese on top. She noticed a glass dish on the bottom shelf of the refrigerator, more funeral food. It looked like lime Jello. She took it out and decided it was, but there were small slices of celery and green peppers in it. There were also some small white lumps in it. She fished one of these out and tasted it—farmer cheese. After trying a bite with all the ingredients, she decided it would go well with their ham biscuits. When Connie saw it on her plate, she wasn't so sure.

"Why does this Jello have lumps in it? And what are they?"

Elizabeth answered, "Cheese."

"Why would you put cheese in Jello?"

"Taste it. It is called a Jello salad. Jack Benny talks about Jello salads on his show."

"I don't know, Betty May. I don't think you are supposed to put cheese in Jello. The Jello is okay, maybe I'll eat around the lumps. The biscuits with the ham are good. Can I have another one?"

Connie washed the few dishes while Elizabeth went upstairs and changed into her pajamas and robe. In the parlor, she turned on the radio and sat on the sofa and pulled her legs up. When Connie finished wiping the table, she said she was going to put on her pajamas too. When she came down, she took her usual position laying across the big ottoman in front of her mother's big chair. She moved two or three times like she could not get comfortable. "This doesn't feel right, Betty May," she said.

"Why don't you sit in Momma's chair."

Connie looked at Elizabeth and considered the heresy she spoke. In a minute, she stood and sat on the edge of her mother's big chair. Slowly she slipped into it and pulled her feet up like Elizabeth's and let the big cushions fold over her. The radio played but neither listened to the show.

"You never said, Betty May. Are we orphans now? Could somebody take our house? Somebody wants it, and I don't like it. Do we have any money? We need money, don't we? If you and Bill get married, will I have to go to an orphan's home?"

Elizabeth turned to her sister in the big chair. She looked small and vulnerable. "Connie, you know and understand so many things I have no idea about. Sometimes I forget you are only ten years old. Yes, I guess we might be considered orphans. But I don't feel like an orphan, do you? What did you feel this afternoon? Who was talking?"

"I don't know who it was, some men in an office. They talked about you and me and Momma and Daddy. I don't think they liked Momma and Daddy. They want to tear down our house."

"We won't let it happen. We do need to be careful. We can make some rules for us. First, we are not going to think of us being orphans, we are a family. And, when Bill and I get married he will be a part of our family. Next, no one is going to take our house. It is ours now, yours and mine. We have to pay our taxes on it and take care of it, but it belongs to us. Daddy showed me about the taxes and paying the light bill last year. It is okay to miss Momma, and Daddy too, I'm going to miss both."

"Betty May, I'm tired. Let's sleep in Momma's bed tonight."

"Yes, let's do."

3

Elizabeth woke and looked around her mother's room. Nothing had been done in there since they returned from New York. Her travel case and overnight bag were in the corner behind the door. Diane had helped her find a burial dress from her mother's closet. They found seven dollars in a pocket of it.

Diane Weston. What would I have done without her? She helped so much getting Momma's body home and arranging for the funeral. I know why Bill liked working with her. With Bill gone, she is the only one...the only one I can trust, my only friend. Bill, Bill, it wasn't supposed to happen this way. You're gone to Boston, Momma's gone to heaven, and I have it all on me.

Tears filled Elizabeth's eyes and she cried quietly.

Twenty minutes later, Connie was still sound asleep with her arms wrapped around a pillow. Elizabeth went downstairs and started a pot of coffee. She found a tablet and a pencil, and from the inside of the pantry door she took down the *O'Neal and Son Pure Oil Service Station* calendar and sat them all in front of her. She read out loud, "November 1946." *I don't guess there will ever be another November like this one.* She put her finger on today, Saturday, November 23. *Only a week left and it's December.* All the dates were big white numbers on a blue background except for 28. Twenty-eight was in outline. *Next Thursday is Thanksgiving. I had completely forgotten. I don't remember a Thanksgiving at home. It is less than a month to Christmas. Oh, Christmas will be so different this year.*

The percolator had been going a few minutes and she turned the stove off. When she lifted the pot, she realized she had made the same amount of coffee she usually made, but from now on, she would be the only one drinking it. *Something else to put on my list.*

Connie came down to the kitchen, she poured a glass of milk. "We need some milk, Betty May."

"We need several things." replied Elizabeth. "Maybe we'll go to town this afternoon. Is there enough milk for cereal?"

"Yes, but I'm hungry this morning. Can't we have bacon and eggs?"

"Connie, if you make do with cereal, maybe we will eat dinner in town at the cafe. We have a lot to do here to get ready for our new life."

"What do we have to do?"

"First, I think we need to unpack Momma's suit cases and put her clothes away."

Connie looked up and started to speak, paused a bit longer and said, "Why Betty May? I know we need to unpack her suitcases, but we don't need to put anything up. And there is all her other stuff. What are we going to do with it?"

"Oh, Connie. You are right. And, Daddy's clothes too, Momma never did anything with his clothes. Everything is still hanging in a closet or in drawers. We need to do something with all of his things."

Connie brought two bowls, the Post Toasties from the cupboard and the jug of milk from the refrigerator. As Elizabeth reached for the jug of milk, Connie extended both hands to her. "Connie, I forgot, we forgot last night." She took Connie's hands and said, "Please say grace for us and ask God to forgive us for forgetting last night."

"Betty May, I've been thinking about Momma's clothes and things. You know she was all the time hiding stuff, money sometimes, and forgetting where she put it. We need to look in all her pockets before we do anything with her clothes.

"We do need to go through all of Momma's clothes. Let's start with the suitcases. We can put everything on the bed in the front bedroom until we decide what to do with it."

By noon, they had been through both suitcases and found $55.35 in pockets, plus a $100 bill between folded underwear. Elizabeth decided to keep her mother's purse, a short mink jacket, two blouses, and the long black silk pants her mother had worn the Saturday night Bill first came to supper. The rest of the clothes were folded and stacked on the bed in the front bedroom.

Sometimes when Connie held something, she would pause and tell Elizabeth what Momma did when she wore the thing last. In a pocket in the big suitcase Connie found a box of small bullets. She put them down like they were hot and said, "Betty May, throw these away. Don't give them to anyone."

"We will drop them in the old privy." Elizabeth answered. "We ought to tear down that old outhouse and fill it anyway. Now, let's get ready and go to town. When we come home, we need to get milk from Mr. Hall so don't let me forget the milk jug."

In fifteen minutes, they were on the road to Greensboro and in another hour and a half they were on their way home. They stopped at the milk house of their neighbor's dairy. Orren Hall sold milk in gallon jugs that had been used for Coca-Cola syrup. Elizabeth put their empty jug in the big sink and pulled a full one from among the big milk cans in the icy water of the cooler, dropping a quarter in the cigar box on the counter. At home, Elizabeth declared it nap time. She got no argument from Connie. This time both went to their own rooms and slept peacefully for the first time since they had taken Bill to Sandy Springs.

It was nearly four o'clock when Elizabeth woke. She heard Connie moving in her room. "Connie, I'm going to Momma's room and work on her chest of drawers. We won't work long, but you can help me by moving things to the front bedroom."

The chest was only four drawers and not high. There was an oval mirror on top. The top drawer was narrow and only contained some small jewelry boxes and a few loose bracelets and rings. A few other boxes and several tied stacks of letters and papers were on one side. *I need to go through this piece by piece. Some of this jewelry may be real. If I can get the drawer out, I'll take it downstairs and start through it tonight.*

"Connie, I might need you to help me carry this downstairs. When I get it out, I'll sit it on the bed, later we'll take it down." Elizabeth pulled the drawer out and turned to the bed.

"Betty May, there is something on the back."

Thumbtacks held an envelope to the drawer. In it were five one-hundred-dollar bills.

Connie looked at the money and said, "We are rich."

"Not really. But Daddy always said you had to have some

cash money handy. So now we do. We really do have to be careful going through Momma's things, and Daddy's too."

"Betty May, it's Saturday. Are we going to dress for Saturday night supper?"

"What if I said no? We are going to have ham sandwiches with store-bought bread and apple salad with pecans. It's not much of a supper to dress for."

"I don't know, Betty May. Saturday supper is another thing we are changing. But I really don't want to change clothes or wash a bunch of dishes after."

Taking the drawer, Elizabeth said, "Okay, ham sandwiches in the kitchen." *But I will have a glass of wine.* Downstairs Elizabeth looked at all the jewelry. She was sure most of it was costume pieces, but there were some rings that could be real. She thought she could take them to Athens or Atlanta and find out. Connie handled each of the pieces but couldn't add anything.

After supper, they both changed into their pajamas and returned to the parlor. Connie had the radio on, and Elizabeth crawled on her sofa and started through the papers in her Momma's drawer. Most were things her mother had written after her sessions—who was there, what happened, and how much she had charged. There was a deed to a house in Sparta in her mother's maiden name, Mary Greene. The next paper she looked at was her parent's marriage license. Elizabeth knew they had been married in Hancock County by the Justice of the Peace. "The date is wrong," she said to no one. "It says December first, 1926. It should be 1925 because they had their twentieth anniversary last year." *If they married in 1926, I would have been born only four months after.* The reality of that thought set in as she remembered last Thursday night with Bill. She rubbed her belly as she let her mind wander to him. A cramp brought her back quickly. *Good, that's something I don't have to worry about now. But Bill, married or not, I am not giving you up.*

4

By late Sunday, Elizabeth and Connie had gone through all their mother's clothes, closets, and drawers. The biggest find of the afternoon was a $50 bill in a box with a matched set of Longine Wittnauer watches. They were gold and looked expensive. The rest of their find was a few dollars in a pocket or an envelope and a $20 bill in the toe of a shoe. The bed in the front bedroom was covered with clothes, from underwear to heavy coats.

"Connie, we have finished Momma's stuff, and I think we are finished for today. All the money is in that shoe box, and all the jewelry is in this one. Count the money for us and write the amount on the side of the box. Later I want you to go through the jewelry and pick out something for you to have."

"Betty May, I want Momma's gold cross. That's all I care about."

"It is yours." Elizabeth knew the cross was valuable, but with Connie's gifts, she didn't see how she could lose it.

"Betty May, it adds to $1,052.64. I did it three times and it came out the same every time. That's a lot, isn't it? Should we put it in the bank?"

"I don't think so. This will be our cash money. I think we can find a safe place for this money, just in case."

"For a rainy day?"

"Yes. I want you to take $52.64 for your rainy-day money. And, I'm going to give you money every week. It will be yours to spend or save."

The telephone rang downstairs. Elizabeth called out, "Bill!" and ran down the front steps and answered before it rang the third time. "Hello...Yes, operator, we will accept the charges...Bill, oh Bill, I have missed you. I love you."

Connie watched and listened for the first few minutes, got bored and went to the parlor and turned on the radio. Connie missed her mother, but decided it was nice to be able to turn on the radio without asking. She heard a final, "I love you." and her sister hang up the phone. But before she came to the parlor, the phone rang again. Connie couldn't hear much of the conversation, but she knew it wasn't Bill and it didn't sound like anything was wrong. In fact, it sounded like her sister was pleased.

"Diane invited us to Thanksgiving dinner at her house. She doesn't have any family close by and wanted us to come. I told her I thought we could. Does it suit you?"

"I think so, Betty May. But I've never had Thanksgiving dinner in a house, only in the big dining room at the Drake. Will there be turkey and stuffing like in New York?"

"Yes. She said she was going to cook a small turkey and dressing."

"What's dressing?"

"I think it is like stuffing, except you don't stuff it inside the turkey. Anyway, I am going to make some biscuits and peach cobbler with our canned peaches and we can make some of the salad we served to Bill when he came to supper."

"You mean the one with the beets and goat cheese."

"Yes."

"I like that, but what did Bill say?"

"Bill was good, but tired. He flew from Atlanta to Dallas on an airliner on Saturday, but his plane was late getting to Dallas and he had to spend the night in the airport and slept on the floor."

"That sounds like fun."

"I don't think he thought it was fun. This morning, the Army sent a plane for him. He knows he is going to be busy, but the best news is he thinks he can come home the week before Christmas and won't have to go back until after New Year's Day. We'll have him for two whole weeks!"

Monday, they started on their Daddy's clothes. Looking into the closet in their parent's bedroom, Elizabeth knew his clothes had not been touched since he died. There wasn't much in the closet though, two suits, two jackets, and a few pairs of trousers. They only found a few coins in a suit coat pocket. His clothes were much too small for Bill, so they decided they were to be given away like their Momma's.

"Connie, let's put everything on the bed in the room where Bill slept. Daddy used the chest of drawers in there where he had his desk. We won't have to move things very far."

There was a small closet in the room, but it only had a few shirts and some work clothes in it. Hanging in the back was a new looking red and green plaid flannel shirt. *This will be a good gift for a certain someone to unwrap on Christmas Eve.* Like her mother's chest, the top drawer of her father's had no clothes, and lowers contained no surprises. Elizabeth pulled the top drawer out and moved toward the bed.

"Nothing on the back," Connie said.

They both noticed his big gold railroad watch with its gold chain. Connie took it and held it for a moment, sniffled, and gave it to Elizabeth. "We need to keep this." she said. As Elizabeth examined her daddy's watch, Connie removed a small cardboard box that had been covered by a brown envelope. She read aloud what was printed on the box, "Trojan Condoms, one dozen, lubricated. Betty May, what are con..." Still holding the box, she never finished her question.

A sound caught in Elizabeth's throat and she looked at her sister who was looking at her holding the box out to her. Neither spoke for several seconds.

"I don't know, Betty May. I think you better keep this. I just don't know."

Elizabeth took the box and set it on top of the chest. "I will take care of this. And we will have a talk soon."

"Things sure are changing."

"Yes, they are, Connie, and we will change too. But maybe not too much and not too fast. One thing that hasn't changed is dirty clothes. We need to take ours to Mary Ison's today. Get yours and we will go before we eat our dinner."

They didn't have so much since their trip to New York had been cut short by their mother's murder. Elizabeth and Connie brought their things to be washed to the kitchen and piled them in the big basket made of strips of white oak woven together. Connie helped Elizabeth carry the basket to the car shed and slide it into the back seat.

Back in the house, Elizabeth sat at her father's desk and went through the papers in the top drawer of his chest. Mostly it was letters from old friends and her father's relatives, and most told about an illness or passing of someone. Elizabeth immediately recognized her mother's small and neat handwriting on two. She read:

September 15, 1926—Sparta.

Dearest Jefferson,
    It is very important I see you here as soon as possible. Do come quickly.

Love,
Mary Greene

Still holding the first, she read the second. It was dated two months later and also from Sparta.

November 16, 1926 — Sparta

Dearest Jefferson,
   Mother passed peacefully in her sleep last night. After the apoplectic fit last week, I knew her time would be soon. I will bury her the day after tomorrow and I know you will not get this before she is buried. No matter. I am alone now, except for you, and alone may be better.
   I have her affairs to settle. Please come when you can.

Love,
Mary Greene

These two letters resolved the "mistake" on her parent's marriage license. There was no mistake. Her parents were married only four and a half months before she was born.

Still holding the two letters, Elizabeth thought about two girls in her dorm her first year at Georgia State. They both left school unexpectedly to get married. When she returned in the fall, she learned both had babies and they both had "come early". Her second year she noticed too there were more girls who got very concerned if they were a little late. She put down the letters and rubbed her cramping belly. *I thought all those girls at school were silly to get in trouble. But Momma wasn't silly and I'm not silly. I don't guess they were either. I want my Bill.* She pulled her heels on the chair and hugged her knees close. *Love sure can get complicated.* After a few minutes she sat, folded the two letters, and put them in her pocket. *These will go to the privy with the bullets. This doesn't matter to anyone now. I will save Daddy's desk for tomorrow.*

Elizabeth fixed bacon and eggs for breakfast. Connie helped with the dishes. "Elizabeth," she said in a serious tone, "are you going to give me lessons like Momma did?"

"I don't think so. You need to go to a real school like you did for four years. I don't think I would be a very good teacher. Besides, I want to go to school too. You remember we talked about getting a little apartment in Athens so I could go to Georgia and you could go to a regular school there. I think all the schools and the university are closed this week for Thanksgiving, but let's plan to go to Athens next week and see what we can find out. We might do some Christmas shopping too."

"I don't think I'm going to like Christmas without Momma and Daddy."

Elizabeth put her arms around her little sister and pulled her close. "Christmas will be different. Remember, Daddy always told us to make the best we could out of everything. Bill will be here."

"I know and I like that, but ..." and Connie's voice trailed off.

"Think about a nice Christmas present you might want. Maybe a radio for your room."

Connie looked curiously at her sister wondering how she could make a radio for her room happen. "I don't know, Betty May. A radio would be pretty big." After a short pause, she continued, "Could we have a Christmas tree?"

Elizabeth smiled. Pleased there was something she could do for her sister's first Christmas without her mother and father, she said, "Yes, we can have a Christmas tree. And maybe, we will have some other decorations too. Now let's go upstairs and work on Daddy's desk. It shouldn't take long."

5

The desk was not large. There were three drawers on the right side of the knee hole with the bottom one being the largest. It was made from a dark wood and it always looked shiny. The matching chair was made from the same dark wood. It was small, but turned and rolled. Elizabeth remembered coming into this room alone when she was five and finding the chair. She sat in it and spun around and around until the seat fell off the base with a loud crash that brought her mother running. She was standing by the chair crying and holding a piece of the arm that had split off. "Betty May, are you hurt?" When she nodded a no, her mother said, "Put the piece down and go downstairs and sit in the parlor. When your father comes home, you must tell him what you did."

Her confession was between sobs and when she had gotten out the gist of the story he simply said, "Show me."

Elizabeth led him to the front stairs and into the bedroom where the chair lay in three pieces on the floor. He looked a minute. "I can fix it." he said as he picked up his daughter. "And, you are not hurt. That's what matters. Let's go eat supper."

Elizabeth wrapped her arms around her daddy's neck, pulled

as close as she could and breathed in the smells that were her daddy.

She and Connie had spent most of the afternoon in the front bedroom the day before and Elizabeth never thought about breaking the chair. But this morning, all that afternoon years ago came back like it happened minutes ago. It took an effort for her to sit in the chair and open the top drawer. It was the smell of wood, pencils, ink, and the remnants of a long-forgotten cigar which floated to her, but it was enough. It was her daddy. She put her face in her hands and cried. It was the first time she cried for her daddy. She hadn't cried when they told her at school, or when she got home or at the funeral. But now it was time. In a few minutes, Connie stood behind the chair. She put her hands on her big sister's shoulders and kissed the top of her head and said, "Daddy knows."

Elizabeth wiped her face with her apron and turned to Connie and kissed her on the cheek. "Thank you. Now, let's see what daddy left us." She pulled the top drawer all the way out. In the front was a little tray with several pencils and a red rubber eraser in it. The tray lifted out and underneath was a block of wood with a circle cut out the size of the bottle of ink that sat there. A black box with a fountain pen and a mechanical pencil sat beside the ink.

Connie took the box with the pen and said, "Daddy liked this pen. He used it to write important things."

Satisfied there was nothing more in the front, Elizabeth removed the polished walnut box which filled most of the rest. The box was heavy. An inscribed silver plate in the center of the top read:

Jefferson Davis DuBose
Twenty-five Years of Loyal Service
Seaboard Air-Line Railroad
July 10, 1944

Elizabeth worked the lock on the front of the box and lifted the lid. Inside was a pistol nested in a red velvet lined cutout. "Seaboard Air-Line Railroad" was engraved on the frame above the trigger. Two boxes of .38 Special cartridges were nested on either side of the revolver and below the barrel was a lid which lifted to reveal several small tools and a cleaning brush.

"That's a gun like Bill had, isn't it, Betty May?"

"I think so. Daddy showed me a gun like this when I was ten. He made me shoot it so I would know how."

"I don't think I like guns. Look in the box. There is a key."

"I don't know this key," Elizabeth said as she picked it up.

Connie wrapped her hand around it and closed her eyes. Her eyes popped wide open. "Betty May, this key is to a money box and the money box is in this house!"

"Do you know where?"

Still clutching the key tightly in her hand, Connie smiled. "It is under the backstairs in the little storeroom beside the back door. Let's go look right now."

Elizabeth stood, "Let's go find Daddy's money box."

To the left of the back door at ground level was the door to a small storeroom that fit under the back stairs. It wasn't large and its ceiling sloped to match the stairs, so the wall was only about four feet high at the back. Elizabeth pulled the door open. "Do you really think Daddy's money box is in here?"

"Yes, it is on the floor."

There was a single light bulb hanging from the ceiling and Elizabeth pulled it on, but it didn't add much to the dark little room. A few garden tools were stacked against one wall. In the middle was a wheel barrow. Sitting on it was a crocus sack full of black walnuts no one had touched since they picked them up in the woods this time last year. "I don't see anything. I'm going to pull the wheel barrow out." Elizabeth took the handles and moved backwards out the door. The steel wheel squeaked on its axle and made a rasping sound as it rolled and skidded across the concrete. "Connie, there is nothing on the floor, see."

"It is in here, Betty May. I know it is." She stood a moment in the middle of the storeroom alternately closing her eyes and looking. "Look there at the back. See how those boards are put together. That's a door and the one board that goes across is the handle." She knelt and pulled on the cross board and the middle of the wall came away. "There it is, Betty May, right there on the floor."

When Elizabeth came closer to look, she blocked the light from the door and from the single bulb. "I can't see." she said.

"Your shadow is in the way. Get down here with me."

"I see it now. Can you get it out?"

Connie reached in and tried to lift the box with no luck. She tried to slide it to her and couldn't move it. "Betty May, this is so full of money, I can't move it. You try."

Elizabeth and Connie swapped places and Elizabeth couldn't move the box either. "I think this box is made to the floor so you can't move it. I can see the place for the key, but it is too dark for me to open it. We need more light."

"Candles, Betty May. Momma's got all those candles in the session room and we don't need them now. Let's go get some." Connie ran to the front room and unlatched the pocket doors to her mother's seance room. She had pushed open the second door when Elizabeth got there, and each took a side of the heavy black drape and pulled it open. Even with the doors and drapes wide open, it was still dark.

Elizabeth saw two big candles under the painting of Jesus. "We will get these." she said. "Bring matches from the kitchen." When she walked out into the front hall, Connie started to pull the drapes closed. "Leave them open. This room needs some light."

"Another change," Connie thought as she headed for the kitchen.

In the storeroom, Elizabeth lit the candles and set one on either side of the box. Kneeling before the box, she waited a moment as her eyes adjusted to the flickering candlelight. Connie stood behind her watching.

"Are you saying a prayer, Betty May?"

"No, but maybe I should. I was waiting until I could see." She put the key in the lock. The key turned easily, and there was a clunk as it stopped. The lid of the box popped open slightly. Elizabeth moved the candles closer and slowly raised the heavy lid.

"What do you see, what's in there?"

Elizabeth held one of the candles to light the box. "It is a tray like in a cash register, you know, with places for different kinds of money. And there is money in it. Maybe a lot of money."

"Can I see?"

"Sure, let me get out."

Elizabeth worked her way backwards on her knees until she could stand. Connie jumped into the opening and squatted. As she settled into position she looked up. "Betty May, there is a light bulb in here." She reached and pulled the string. Light filled the opening. Connie looked at the box. "Whoa! There is a lot of money. She reached down to a stack of bills. As she touched the tray it slid back. "I think this tray thing comes out. Yes, there is a wire handle in the middle." She lifted it up and away. "Betty May, this box is deep. It is made into the floor and there is lots of stuff down in it."

Elizabeth took the tray from Connie.

"There is more money in here." She reached in and one by one brought out four bundles of bills each wrapped with a paper and held together with a rubber band. As she handed the bundles to Elizabeth, she said, "That's a lot of money, isn't it?"

"Yes, it sure looks like it."

"There's more," Connie said as she handed Elizabeth five more bundles. "I think this is all the money. I see a bunch of papers tied with a string and a little leather bag. It is kind of heavy." she said as she handed the bag to Elizabeth. "What's in there?"

"It is tied tight at the top. We'll have to wait until we get inside to look. Can you reach the papers?"

"Here," and she handed a stack of letters and other papers held together with a lace. "That's all I see in here."

"Good. We need to take all this inside and see what we have. With a little effort they got the secret door in place and rolled in the old wheel barrow. Elizabeth put the bundles of bills into the pockets of her overalls. Connie took the leather bag and the bundle of papers.

At the kitchen table, Elizabeth picked up one of the bundles. The rubber band crumpled and fell off. She opened the paper and recognized her father's handwriting. *This looks like Daddy sold some things. Here's the price and date. These must be expenses: rent, labor, freight. These are initials. JDD, that's the way Daddy always did his initials. It looks like the money was divided four ways: JDD, HT, JH and HDG, and each got $1550.37.*

"Fourteen hundred eighty, fifteen hundred. That's close," Elizabeth said as she looked at the paper. "Oh, I see. He wrote $50.37 and put a circle around it, so that much is not in the stack." She handed the paper to her sister. "Can you tell anything about this?"

Connie looked at the paper, "Daddy wrote this. He wrote it with his pen because it was important."

"How about these letters?" Elizabeth pointed to the ones she thought were initials.

"I don't know what they are, but I don't like them, except the first one. It makes me think of Daddy."

"I'm not sure what they are either, but I think these are Daddy's initials. I think the others are initials for other people. Count the money in the tray while I count these."

Connie had stacked the bills from the tray in piles and made a list that she added. "Betty May, it is $3,055. How much do you have?"

"$17,250."

"Whoa!"

"With what you have there and Momma's money we found yesterday, we have over $21,000. It really is a lot of money. It doesn't make us forever rich, but it is enough for us to go to Athens and go to school. And, I will save enough for you to go to college too."

"Should we put this in the bank?"

"I don't think so, not right now. Daddy kept this money hidden for a reason, and I think we should too. He had it in a good hiding place. I want to go through these letters and papers. Oh, let's open this leather bag. I wonder what's in it."

Elizabeth worked at the lace. "I see some money in here, and it is coins." She turned the bag and carefully poured its contents on the desktop. There were coins, gold ones, a gold bracelet that looked like it was made for a man, a small cardboard box and a key. "These coins are gold, real gold, and I am sure this bracelet is real gold too. See how heavy it is. The coins say they are twenty dollars, but I think they are worth more." She opened the cardboard box. "Jewels," she said. "These must be real or Daddy wouldn't have kept them."

"Can I hold one?"

"Be careful, some of the diamonds are small."

Connie held the largest green stone. "This is really pretty, but I don't know anything about it." She examined several more stones one at a time. "Betty May, I think they are real, but I don't know where they came from or anything about them." She took the key, "This is Momma's." She read from one side, "The Bank of Sparta." A pause, "There's a number on it. It is for a money box too, but I think it is in that bank."

"I found a paper saying Momma owned a house in Sparta. When Bill gets here maybe we can go there and find out about the house and the key. I am going to save the letters we found in the box for later. Let's put this key with the money box key and put the rest of this back in the bag." Elizabeth spent another hour going through the desk drawers. There were letters from Seaboard and from the Drake Hotel, but nothing else seemed important right now.

Connie had become bored with Elizabeth's announcements about what letter or paper she had found and had gone downstairs to listen to the radio. Elizabeth called to her. "We are going to put all of this in the money box. Where should we hide the key?"

"Don't hide it. If we hide it and somebody finds it, they'll think it is important and go looking for what it opens. Like we did. But if it is out, anybody who saw it wouldn't think anything of it. Momma always hung her house key on the nail in the pantry where she hung her apron. Put it there."

After they put all the money and the leather bag in the money box, they put everything together in the store room, and Elizabeth hung the key on the nail in the pantry and covered it with her mother's apron. "Let's eat." she said and fixed them a sandwich for their dinner. After, they both nodded off in the parlor.

6

Connie was sleeping soundly in her mother's chair when Elizabeth woke. The afternoon light showed dust on the table at the end of the sofa. *We've kept up with the dishes, but I know the floor in the kitchen is dirty and the front hall needs sweeping. Connie's room? I haven't been in there. It could be a mess. Momma made us do little things, but she did so much herself. This house is a big job. If we go to Athens to school, nothing will get done here and I'll have to take care of where we stay in Athens.*

Elizabeth stood and walked to the kitchen and fixed a glass of tea. *And there is the land. We only have twenty-five acres, but Daddy had people to come and cut hay, and Moses did odd jobs. I don't know anything about that. At least Bill does, he grew up on a farm. Oh, I do so need my Bill right now.*

After a sip of tea, she went to her room. *At least money is not a problem. We have enough to last until Bill and I get married, or I can get a job. And, we'll have some money coming in from Daddy's investments. They were going to send a check to Momma on December first. I'll bet they don't know Momma's dead. Can I cash her check? I've been writing checks for her since Daddy died and signing her name. I can't sign any more. I need to call Mr. Harwell and find out, and I need to call the broker in New York, too. This gets harder and harder. I'm Connie's sister, not her mother, I can tell her some things, but she really needs a mother and she doesn't know it. Hell, I need a mother. It is only 2:15, I'll call our broker in New York and make sure he knows about Momma.*

In a few minutes she was speaking with Mr. Ward, the man she had spent the morning with the day before her mother was killed. He knew nothing of her mother's death and sounded a bit relieved to know Elizabeth and Connie had no immediate need for money. "Miss DuBose", he asked, "did your mother have a will, and who is to be the executor for your mother's estate?"

Elizabeth replied, "I am sure she did not have a will, and I guess I am."

After a short pause when Elizabeth heard papers shuffling, Mr. Ward continued, "Miss DuBose, I see you are not yet 21 years old and, in fact, won't be until 1948. In New York, a minor can't be an executor and I suspect the same is true in Georgia. The Probate Court will have to appoint someone to handle your mother's affairs. Do you have a close relative who could do that?"

"No, we have no relatives."

"One moment, Miss DuBose. I see in the file a man named Hiram Tilley is the Clerk for Greene County. I take it you haven't talked with him. Do you know him?"

"I know who he is, but he is not a friend, and I haven't talked with him."

"It appears Mr. Tilley suggested your mother to be the executor for your father's estate, and a Judge Morrow approved the appointment. I think you get in touch with Mr. Tilley right away and get started on having an executor appointed. As an unmarried minor, there is very little I can do with you. When one is appointed, please have him get in touch with me."

"I will, Mr. Ward. Goodbye."

Connie walked into the hall and looked at Elizabeth, "What's the matter? You are really mad."

"That man in New York that has Daddy's money, no, our money, thinks I can't take care of it and you. He says a judge will need to appoint somebody to take care of you."

"Why?"

"Because I am not twenty-one and a girl—that Yankee son of a bitch."

"You are mad, Betty May. Does he want our house? I told you somebody wants our house."

"Well I don't think it is him."

"You can take care of us. I know you can."

"I can if you help me, we can get along just fine. Let's do a little housework this afternoon and tomorrow we will get our food ready to go to Thanksgiving dinner at Diane's house. If you go clean your room, I will sweep downstairs." *I'm going to wait until I talk with Diane before I call Mr. Tilley. She ought to know him and something about what he does.*

Elizabeth was up early on Wednesday. She fixed coffee, it didn't take long for one person. While it was percolating, she went to her room and brought down all the information she had from the University of Georgia. After reading through it, it was clear she had been admitted and was expected in September. She realized she had never done anything to let the people at Georgia know she was not coming. And she was sure her mother had not as well.

There was a letter from the dean welcoming her to the University of Georgia. It had his name and telephone number on it. *I'll call this morning, but I doubt I will get anyone. If I do, I can make an appointment for next week.* At nine-thirty she called, and as expected, Dean Truitt was not going to be in until Monday. Elizabeth explained why she was calling, and the lady said the dean could see her at eleven on Tuesday, and she would find Elizabeth's file and put it on the dean's desk first thing Monday morning.

"Connie," Elizabeth said, "we are going to Athens and the University of Georgia on Tuesday."

"Are you going to school?"

"Not on Tuesday, but I am going to talk to the dean and see if I can start. After seeing him we can go in town and do some Christmas shopping. How would that be?"

"Who is Dean?"

"Dean is not his name, it's like his job. Like doctor or professor."

"Well, dean is a funny name for somebody who lets you go to school."

Elizabeth fixed the peach cobbler to take to Diane's and Connie swept and dusted her mother's room. In the process, she found another thirty dollars in a Bible on her mother's nightstand. Elizabeth told her to add it to her rainy-day money.

They slept a little later Thursday morning. After breakfast, Elizabeth bathed and found what she was going to wear to Diane's. She helped Connie pick out an outfit. Connie was determined to wear her mother's gold cross even though it looked too big for her.

Thanksgiving dinner was different in Diane's small home, but both Elizabeth and Connie enjoyed being with a friend. Diane had asked Pete Moss who worked at the funeral home to join them. Diane said he didn't have any kin close by and she didn't want him to have to spend Thanksgiving in an empty funeral home.

Elizabeth told Diane what the broker said about having someone appointed to handle her business because she wasn't twenty-one. Diane agreed he was probably right but said she would ask the sheriff and maybe her friend, Mary, in Judge Morrow's office. She said she knew Hiram Tilley but didn't think much of him.

Riding home, Connie said, "Pete is Diane's boyfriend. She likes him a lot."

"You are a treasure."

As they reached the beginning of their property, Elizabeth looked at the fence. A thunderstorm in the late summer had brought down a pine tree that fell across the fence. If her mother ever noticed it, she never mentioned it, and Elizabeth didn't think about it either. But today, Elizabeth realized it was her fence and her responsibility. If she were going to take care of Connie and the house, this was something needing her attention. *When Bill calls, I'll ask him. No, no I won't. Mr. Hall knows about fences. Or Moses and Travis can fix it. I'll take care of this myself.*

"See where the fence is down. I need to get it fixed. There may be some more things around the house that need work. Tell me if you see something."

"Betty May, the gate in behind the car shed is broken in two. Is that what you're talking about?"

"Yes, it is. I'll add it to my list."

Bill called late. Elizabeth could tell he was excited about all that was going on and seemed to be happy about being in the Army again.

The words poured out of Bill's mouth, "Next week, I will be flying a different plane every day. Some I've flown before, but there are two I haven't. I'll have to study all weekend to get ready for them."

For the first time, Elizabeth realized she would compete with flying and the Army. Bill talked about their last night together and waking up in the bed they had shared. "Elizabeth May Du-Bose, wedding or not, you are part of me. I love you."

"I love you, too, and I want you home. Some things have happened you need to know about."

Bill understood about appointing an executor for Mary Greene's estate. He said he didn't think it would make much difference until he remembered Hiram Tilley would be involved. "I've never quite trusted him. He never seemed to be trying to help anyone but himself."

"Diane said she knew him but didn't know much about what he did. She was going to talk to the sheriff at work tomorrow."

"Good. There is a guy here who went to law school in South Carolina. I'll ask him about what could happen. In the meantime, keep track of everything. Do you need any money?"

"No, we found some Momma and Daddy had hidden. It is enough."

"Will it be safe if you don't put it in the bank?"

"I think so. It took Connie's gift to find it, and we put it in the same place."

"It will be safe enough. Have you paid Fred for the funeral? And, how about taxes."

"I know I have those things to do, but I haven't paid for the funeral yet. The tax bills don't come until the first of December. I am going to the post office on Monday. I will pay both while we are in town."

"Elizabeth, I'm thinking, the bank account is in your mother's name, right?"

"Yes, it was in Daddy's name and Momma had to sign a lot of papers to get it in her name. I remember now, she didn't care for Mr. Tilley because of what he made her do. For the past six months, I have signed her name on checks, and no one said anything. I don't think I can do that anymore."

"I think you are right."

"Bill, Connie and I talked about going to school. She needs to be in school and I think another town would be good for her. I have an appointment to talk to the dean at Georgia on Tuesday. What do you think?"

"I think that's good. You are right, Connie needs to be in a regular school, and you need to be in college. I will talk to my friend and call you again on Sunday night."

"Bill, I miss you so. I want you here in my arms, and in our bed."

7

Friday morning, Elizabeth and Connie drove down to Moses' cabin. He and Liza came out as soon as they saw the car.

"Miss Elizabeth, Miss Cornelia, Good morning. We hope you are well."

Connie ran around to the side where Moses and Liza were. "Good morning," she said, "We've come to tell you about Momma's and Daddy's clothes."

"Yes'm," Moses answered.

"Connie and I hoped you or folks in your church might have use for some of Momma's and Daddy's clothes. There is nothing we can use, and Daddy's clothes are too small for Bill. Do you want them, and can you come get them?"

Moses said, "Yes ma'am, we'd be pleased for anything, and they would be put to good use. Yes'm, we'll come any time you say. Thank you."

"Bless you both," said Liza, "and thank you."

"Good," said Elizabeth. "Moses, do you know where the tree fell last summer and knocked down part of the fence?"

"Yes'm."

"Can you fix that? Do you know how?"

"Me and Travis can fix the fence. There be other places needing attention if you want."

"Yes, I would appreciate that. Please look around and let me know what needs work and tell me if you need money for supplies."

"Yes'm., I will. If it suit, I'll look around the place and see what's there. Your daddy kept good supplies and tools."

"That will be fine. There is a wheel barrow and some garden tools in the store room by the back door. I'll move them to the car shed. Don't go in the store room. We are going to use it for something else."

"Yes'm. Miz Elizabeth, do you need any help with the house? Inside help, cleaning and washing, I mean. Travis' Clara could work some for you iffen you like."

"Oh, yes. Good. I'm afraid Momma let things get ahead of her. Yes, Clara's help would be good. Can you come tomorrow afternoon to get the clothes? And, we can talk about the other things."

"Yes'm, we will be there."

"Where are we going now?" Connie asked as they passed the turn to their home.

"We are going to the funeral home to pay Mr. Thompson, and to the post office. I want to talk to Diane at the sheriff's office too."

"Can we eat lunch at the cafe, or a hot dog at Hunter's?"

"Lunch? Sure, we can have 'lunch' in town."

As expected, there was no mail in their box, so Elizabeth

went to the window. "Mr. Jeffcoat, I want to get our mail, and let you know not to hold it any longer."

"Just a moment, Miss DuBose," he replied. Turning, he called, "Donald, Miss DuBose is here for their mail. Do you have it in the back?"

A voice answered, "I will be right out."

Mr. Jeffcoat started to relay the message, but Elizabeth said, "I heard him."

Donald Conway came empty handed. "Miss DuBose, Connie, we are sorry about your mother. You have our deepest sympathies."

"Thank you, Mr. Conway. May I get our mail?"

"Miss DuBose, if there was anything addressed to you or to Connie, you could have those. Everything I am holding is addressed to your mother, and some to your father. Since they are deceased, I must hold it until the estate is established."

"But there may be business matters I need to take care of," Elizabeth said.

"It shouldn't take long to appoint an executor, and he can go through your mother's mail for you."

Elizabeth felt Connie step closer, and she knew Connie was going to speak. She quickly turned and put her hand on Connie's lips and said, "We must go right now. This will wait." She turned to Mr. Conway and said, "That will be all for now." She took Connie's hand and walked quickly from the post office.

In the car, Connie said, "Betty May, you are angry."

"I am. I am as mad as hell. I don't know why the stupid son of a bitch won't give us our mail. He doesn't have anything to do with an executor. Something's not right."

"Betty May, please don't swear. Momma didn't like for Daddy to swear. But I know why you are angry. The Post Office man was not telling the truth about our mail. I don't know why, but he wasn't."

"You are right I don't need to swear, but we need to find out what's going on." Elizabeth drove around the block and down past where Bill's garage apartment had been behind the McLean's house. Finally, she said, "We'll go pay Mr. Thompson for the funeral."

"What's got y'all out and in town this morning?" Diane asked as Elizabeth and Connie entered the sheriff's office.

"We are on some errands, but I do have a question for you."

Sheriff DeWitt said, "Good morning, ladies. Elizabeth, have you heard from Bill?"

"Yes, he called last night." And she told the sheriff and Diane about Bill.

After Elizabeth answered more questions, she said, "Sheriff, I have a question about my mother's estate." She told about the conversation she had with their New York broker. "Do I have to have someone take care of our business? I've been taking care of everything for my mother since daddy died."

"When will you be twenty-one?"

"Not until March in 1948."

"Since you're not twenty-one, the court, the probate court, will need to appoint someone of legal age to act for you. I don't know of any relatives you have. Is there anyone?"

"No. How about Bill? We are engaged."

"I doubt Judge Morrow would go along with Bill because he is so far away. Whoever is appointed needs to be close by to sign papers and so forth."

"Sheriff DeWitt, how about you or Diane? I trust both of you."

"The judge doesn't like to appoint county employees unless they are close relatives. I don't think either of us would do. John Harwell is somebody the judge has appointed before. He is someone who has an idea about your estate already."

"I guess he'd be okay. I need to do something soon. They wouldn't give me our mail when I stopped at the post office."

"Who wouldn't?"

"Mr. Conway."

"Do you have anything else to do in town this morning?"

"Not much. We paid Mr. Thompson. We need some things from the Big Store for the house, and we were going to eat dinner at the cafe."

"Do you have any other money? Cash at home for food and everyday things?"

Elizabeth put her arm around Connie's shoulder and pulled her close. Looking at the sheriff, she said, "Connie and I have a little of our rainy-day money, and Momma kept a few dollars for groceries. We have enough for a while." She paused and added, "I had fixed an envelope with the money for the taxes. The tax bill is one thing I wanted from the mail."

Sheriff DeWitt said, "For right now, remember your rainy-day money is your money and not part of the estate. Do your other errands but stop here before you head home."

Diane was the only one in the sheriff's office when they came after they ate.

"Is Sheriff DeWitt here?"

"No, he's gone home to dinner, but here is your mail. He said to tell you all your mail would be in the box from now on."

"Tell him thanks, but what did he do?" Elizabeth asked.

"There are some things I don't ask about." Diane replied. "And, there are some things he doesn't ask me about either."

"I told you the man at the Post Office wasn't telling the truth," Connie added.

"Diane, have you found out about Hiram Tilley?"

"He's the County Clerk. I guess his biggest job is to collect taxes. When somebody dies, he always makes sure the county gets paid first for taxes. He's not the most popular boss in the courthouse."

"I guess I need to go and see him."

"I heard somebody say he was off today, but I wouldn't hurry. Let him get in touch with you."

"We enjoyed dinner yesterday. I think Connie and I needed a day with friends. I saw Pete when we paid Mr. Thompson. He seems really nice."

"You like him a lot," Connie said.

"Yes, I do Connie," Diane answered. "Now I understand what Bill meant when he said you knew things you had no reason to know."

In the car, Elizabeth went through the envelopes. "This looks like it might be the tax bill," she said as she opened the envelope in her hand. "Yes, and I have enough to pay it now. Let's go do that while Mr. Tilley is not there, and we won't have any reason to come again to the courthouse."

Saturday morning was cold and rainy. Elizabeth set Connie to going through her closet for outgrown clothes and adding them to the stack in the front bedroom. "Tomorrow, you and I are going to get our rooms clean and neat," she told Connie.

"But, Betty May, you shouldn't work on Sunday."

"Connie, the Lord doesn't love ugly or dirty. He won't mind if we clean. And, I don't want somebody like Mr. Tilley coming in our house and thinking we can't take care of it."

"Me neither. I don't think I like Mr. Tilley."

"He might just be doing his job, we need to do ours."

After dinner, it seemed to be colder. Moses, Liza, Travis, and Clara came in two wagons and pulled to the back door. Travis and Clara made the trips between the upstairs bedrooms with the piles of clothes, and Moses and Liza loaded them from the kitchen into the wagons. Even though the rain had stopped, they covered everything with quilts.

When the wagons were loaded, Liza said, "Miss Elizabeth, Miss Cornelia, thank you for these clothes. They be a blessing."

"You're welcome, Liza. We are glad they can be used. Now let's sit down in the parlor and talk a minute."

Moses spoke first. "Miss Elizabeth, I can come Monday evening and see if there is anything we need from town to start on the fences. Me and Travis can start Tuesday morning early."

"Good, Moses," Elizabeth replied. "Connie and I are going to Athens on Tuesday and will be gone most of the day."

"You don't mind us being here while you are gone?" Moses asked.

"Not at all, Moses. Clara, could you come on Tuesday too?"

"Yes'm."

"Miss Elizabeth," Liza asked, "do you mind if I come and bring the baby? I could help Clara some, and we could go over the house real good."

"Oh, that would be wonderful."

Before supper, Elizabeth went to the pantry to get a bottle of wine for the bar. "This is the last bottle of Daddy's wine. I know where he bought it in Athens. We'll stop there on the way home on Tuesday."

Sunday was cold, the coldest day of the fall. Elizabeth and Connie slept late and ate toasted biscuits and ham for breakfast. After they straightened the kitchen from their breakfast and last night's supper, Connie went to her room, and Elizabeth read through more of the letters they had found. Elizabeth was holding one of her mother's letters in her hand. She wasn't reading it, she was thinking about Bill and the things she had to tell him. He said he would wait until six o'clock when the rates changed.

"Betty May," Connie's voice brought her back. "If I'm going to school in Athens, I might need some new clothes. We were going to buy some things in New York."

"New York clothes might not be right for Athens," Elizabeth answered, "but Greensboro clothes might not be either. Yes, you do need some new clothes. We will go to Gallant-Belk and see what we can find. I might need some new things too."

Sunday afternoon dragged on. When Bill hadn't called by six-thirty, Elizabeth began to pace into the hall every few minutes.

Connie said, "He'll call, don't worry."

"I know," Elizabeth answered. "I think I'll have a glass of wine." She sipped her wine until seven and walked into the hall and stared at the telephone. It didn't ring. In the parlor, she poured another glass of wine.

Connie said, "Don't worry, nothing is wrong, and I'm hungry. Can I fix a hot dog?"

"Yes. Put them in the big pot and..."

"I know how," Connie interrupted. "Do you want one?"

"I guess, and we have some potato chips."

"Betty May, sit and watch the telephone, I will fix our supper."

The only thing the hot dog supper did for Elizabeth was to pass some time and upset her stomach. At eight o'clock, she couldn't wait any longer. "Connie, I have to go to the bathroom. If the phone rings answer it."

In a moment the phone rang, and Connie answered, "Hello Bill, Betty May is in the bathroom, and she is mad you didn't call at six o'clock, and it is after eight now. I told her you were all right."

"Connie, it is only six o'clock where I am in New Mexico," Bill replied.

"I think your clock must be broken. It is after eight. The man on the radio said so."

"I will explain it when I come home. Tell Elizabeth I'm on the phone."

"She knows, I heard the toilet."

"Bill," Elizabeth called as she took the receiver from Connie. They talked a few minutes about the time difference and about missing and loving each other. Elizabeth said, "Bill, I'm worried about having somebody take over Momma's money and the house."

Bill said, "I talked to the guy here who had been to law school. He said the court would have to appoint someone. Do you think it could be me?"

"Sheriff DeWitt said he didn't think you could be it because you would be too far away and couldn't sign things. When can you come home?"

"I won't be there for nearly two weeks. I'll get to Boston next weekend, and I'll have to register and find a place to live. The Army has left it all to me. From now on, all my flying will be military, so I won't know a schedule."

8

About eleven o'clock, Hiram Tilley walked from his office toward the stairs. As he passed the counter, Margaret called out, "Mr. Tilley."

"Yes."

"I thought you might want to know Elizabeth DuBose came in on Friday and paid the taxes for their place."

"Didn't I tell you to not take a payment unless they had the bill?" he snapped.

"Yes sir," Margaret replied, "but she had the tax bill."

"What?"

"Elizabeth had the bill we mailed last week. I remember what you said, but she had their tax bill and the cash money to pay it. I didn't know what else to do."

Margaret caught a "son of a bitch" in Tilley's mumbling, and, "I'm going to the post office, to the bank, and dinner."

"I know what you said, Hiram," the postmaster replied. "But Ben came in and told me I didn't have any right to withhold the Du-

Bose's mail. He was still pissed about me holding a letter for his deputy. I gave it all to him."

Angry, Tilley asked, "Donald, don't you think giving the sheriff somebody else's mail without a warrant is a crime?"

"Tell you what, Hiram, you take all of this up with Sheriff Ben DeWitt and let me know how it turns out. Meantime, I'm gonna run the post office."

"Shit," mumbled Tilley as he walked out of the post office toward the Harwell Bank.

"Don't worry about it, Hiram," Harwell said. "We would have had to pay the taxes anyway. Her mother's account has plenty for that. Fred told me Elizabeth came by Friday and paid cash for the funeral."

"Damn," Tilley replied. "I sure would like to get a handle on things so we can get into the house."

"I know. The more cash she uses now the sooner she'll be here for her mother's money. Elizabeth is smart, she'll understand about having to have an executor."

"I know she's smart, and they say the young one has visions. I want to get all of this done before they figure out what's happening. I'm going out there tomorrow and talk to Elizabeth."

"Hiram, be nice and act like you want to be helpful, and don't do anything to get Ben DeWitt involved."

"Connie, are you about ready? I can't be late for my meeting with Dean Truitt."

"I'm ready, and I'm going to take some of my money for Christmas shopping."

The drive to Athens was quick and Elizabeth found the Dean's office without trouble. While they waited, Elizabeth and Connie told the dean's secretary, Mrs. Rollins, a little about their situation.

"Oh, I am so sorry about your mother, and your father. You two have been through a lot. Are you going to live in Athens?"

"Yes," Elizabeth replied. "We will keep our house in Greensboro, but we would like to get an apartment here so Connie could go to school too."

With a big smile, Mrs. Rollins said, "I know the place for you. It is a garage apartment with two bedrooms—close to campus and close to Barrow Elementary School for Connie. Here is the owner's name. I'll call her if you want to go see it."

"Yes, we would like that," Elizabeth answered as Dean Truitt came to his door.

"Come in," he said.

In thirty minutes, he had Elizabeth enrolled for the winter quarter. "Classes don't start until January seventh this year. Here are your professor's names and where the classes will be. Go to the book store before classes start and get your books and take this to the Bursar's Office. Since you won't be in a dorm room, you are due a refund."

"Thank you, sir," Elizabeth answered.

"Welcome to the University of Georgia."

About ten o'clock, Hiram Tilley turned onto Godfrey's Store Road. In no hurry, he went over how he would tell Elizabeth about selecting an executor for her mother's estate and a guardian for her and her sister. As he neared the house, he saw a colored man working a mule to pull a fallen tree away from the barbed wire fence. *That's DuBose property he's on. What the hell is he doing?*

At the house, he saw a team and wagon by the car shed behind the house. Moses Jackson walked from the shed carrying a spool of barbed wire.

"Boy," Tilley called out. "What are you doing?"

"Sir," Moses replied, dipping his head slightly. "Me and my son is fixin' Miss DuBose fence down by the road. This here is some wire Mr. DuBose had."

"Does Miss DuBose know you're plundering through the car shed?"

"Oh, yes sir," Moses answered as he put the wire in the wagon. "She said to find what we needed in the shed so she wouldn't have to buy anything."

"Mind what you take," Tilley answered as he turned toward the house.

"Yes sir, Mr. Tilley, sir," Moses said. "Miss Elizabeth and Miss Cornelia aren't here. They gone to Athens."

"How do you know my name, boy? When are they coming back?"

"Mr. Tilley, I see you at the court house. You are the tax man. Miss DuBose didn't tell me when she would be home, but they left early this morning."

Seeing a movement at the kitchen window, Tilley asked, "Who is inside?"

"Sir, my wife and my son's wife are cleaning for Miss DuBose."

"Damn," Tilley said under his breath as he walked to his car. He wrote something and put the paper in an envelope. "I'm going to leave this in the front door for Miss DuBose. It is important. Don't bother it."

"Oh, no sir, we wouldn't touch it at all. But, Mr. Tilley, Miss Elizabeth and Miss Cornelia don't hardly go and come by the front door, especially when they be driving. I'd be pleased to give it to my wife. She could put it on the table in the kitchen."

"You do that. If you see them when they come home, tell them I was here."

"Yes sir, Mr. Tilley."

The apartment suited Connie and Elizabeth. It was over a three-car garage and had one room across the front with a kitchen at one end and two small bedrooms on the back with a bathroom between.

"The bathroom only has a shower," Connie said. "I like showers."

"I like showers too," Elizabeth said to Connie. Turning to Mrs. Creech, she said, "We would like to rent this. What do we need to do?"

"If you want it starting January first, I'll want the rent in advance and another month's rent as a deposit, and it is yours. Do you want to move in sooner?"

"No, the first will be fine. My fiancé will be here, and he can help move some things over before he has to return to Boston. I will have to come tomorrow with the rent and deposit."

Mrs. Creech looked toward her house and said, "I guess I will hold it for you until tomorrow afternoon. Even if he is your fiancé, I don't allow unmarried women to have overnight male guests."

Connie started to speak and got out, "Bill sleeps..." when Elizabeth's hand touched her shoulder, and she stopped.

"I understand," Elizabeth said. "We will be here tomorrow. Thank you, Mrs. Creech."

"Now, Connie, we will go to your school and get you enrolled."

"Ask to see Mr. Price. He is the principal," Mrs. Creech said as Elizabeth and Connie walked to the car.

At Barrow Elementary, Mr. Price wanted the whole story of Elizabeth and Connie's recent life. Finally, he said, "Elizabeth, I will go ahead and get things started for Connie to start in January, but I will need to have her legal guardian sign some of the papers. Who is he?"

Elizabeth paused, "Mr. Price, everything has happened so fast the court has not appointed anyone yet. I'm sure it will be done before the end of the month."

Mr. Price gave Elizabeth and Connie a quick tour of the school which ended out front under the arches. A line of children came from the side toward the doors. Mr. Price said, "Connie, those are your classmates, fifth grade."

Elizabeth started the car, "Let's wait until tomorrow to shop. We have to come to pay Mrs. Creech, and we will have plenty of time."

"Okay, but you are kinda mad, Betty May. Why?"

"Connie, nobody thinks I can take care of you, of us. They all want to tell me what to do because I am a girl and not twenty-one."

On the outskirts of Athens, Elizabeth stopped at the liquor store where her daddy and momma bought wine. Connie got out and joined Elizabeth as they entered.

The clerk looked from behind the counter as the bell on the door jingled. "Children can't come in here," he called out.

"She is with me," Elizabeth answered.

The clerk walked out and said, "And, how old are you?"

"I'm nineteen."

"Like I said, children can't come in here. You have to be twenty-one. Now, run along."

Elizabeth slammed the car door, sat holding the steering wheel and looked straight ahead with tears in her eyes. Connie didn't speak.

"God damn it all," Elizabeth almost yelled, "I can't even buy a fucking bottle of wine. Shit!" Without another word, she started the car and headed toward Greensboro.

9

The smell of pine cleaner and furniture polish welcomed them into their house. It was a clean smell, a good smell, one they had almost forgotten. Elizabeth turned on the kitchen light.

"Whoa," Connie called out, "it's sparkly in here."

"Clara and Liza did a good job," Elizabeth answered. "Momma let things get behind. I can't let it happen again. What's on the table?"

Connie lifted a cloth covering a plate and bowl on the kitchen table. "Supper," she said. "Ham, potato salad, and biscuits. Liza must have fixed this for us. Here's a letter, too." As she reached for the plain white envelope, she said, "It says 'DuBose children'."

"Let me see."

As soon as Connie touched the envelope, she moaned. "This is bad, Betty May. This is from the man who wants our house," and she dropped the envelope on the table. "Burn it, Betty May. Burn it."

Elizabeth read the penciled note inside. "This is from the man at the court house, Mr. Tilley. He says we have to come to see him tomorrow about Momma's estate and her affairs."

"He's lying, Betty May. He wants our house."

"Connie, I think we are going to have to go and see him, but we won't go tomorrow. We are going to Athens to pay Mrs. Creech and go shopping for our new school clothes. Yes, Mr. Tilley can wait for us."

"Make him wait a long time, Betty May."

"We'll see. When we saw the children at the school, did you see any clothes you liked?"

"I did. There were some pretty dresses, and none of the boys had on overalls."

Connie and Elizabeth didn't start for Athens until after nine o'clock. Elizabeth had taken three hundred dollars from her daddy's box in the storeroom. *Fifty- and hundred-dollar bills will cause talk in Greensboro. If I go to a bank in Athens, I can get change, and the department stores won't have a problem with the big bills.* After stopping at the Hubert Banking Company and getting change for the hundred-dollar bill, they went to Mrs. Creech's home and paid her $36 for two month's rent.

Riding home to Greensboro, Connie said, "Betty May, this is the most new clothes I have ever had at one time."

"We are going to have a new life in a new place. New clothes are going to be a part of our change."

"I know, but I feel selfish. I didn't buy a Christmas present for you or for Bill. I should have done that."

"Connie, you always bring me to what's right. I didn't do any Christmas shopping either. I guess we need to come to Athens on Friday and Christmas shop."

"Betty May, I don't want to go see that Tilley man. Why don't you go by yourself?"

"I want him to see us as a family, and besides, you always have feelings about people. I want you to tell me what you think about him. But not while we are there, later when we are alone."

Virginia asked Connie and Elizabeth to have a seat, and she knocked and went into Mr. Tilley's office. When she came out, Mr. Tilley was standing behind her. "Miss DuBose, please come in. We have some important things to discuss."

Elizabeth stood and motioned Connie to stand and they both stepped toward the door.

"Just you, Miss DuBose. The young one has no need to hear what I have to tell you," said Mr. Tilley.

"Mr. Tilley, Connie and I only have each other right now, so anything you have to say to me, you can say to her. We are in this together." Elizabeth took Connie's hand and they walked past Mr. Tilley into his office and sat in the two chairs opposite his desk.

Tilley closed the door and stood behind his desk. "Children," he said, "it is my job to make sure all the obligations of your mother's estate are met, and you two, her orphan children, are properly supervised and cared for."

Connie had not taken her eyes from Mr. Tilley's since they entered the room. Elizabeth sensed she was about to stand and speak, so she reached over and put her hand on the arm of Connie's chair. Connie settled, but continued to keep her eyes directly on Tilley's.

He continued, "Miss DuBose, you are old enough you don't have to have a guardian, but your sister..."

"My sister's name is Cornelia. We call her Connie, you may too. And Mr. Tilley, please speak to her if you have something…"

"I'm Miss DuBose, too," Connie said.

Mr. Tilley paused and continued, "Yes, well Miss Cornelia you must have a guardian who can make decisions about your care. Since your sister, Miss Elizabeth, is not yet twenty-one years old, she can't be a guardian. Do you understand?"

"We understand what you said, Mr. Tilley."

"Good, and we need someone to be responsible for the affairs of your mother's estate."

"Who do you plan to appoint?" Elizabeth asked. "And when?"

"Miss DuBose," a pause, "both of you, I don't appoint. Judge Morrow in Crawfordville will make the appointments, but I am going to suggest he appoint John Harwell as both guardian and executor. He is someone you know well, isn't he?"

"Of course, we know Mr. Harwell. But I suggest my fiancé, William Brown. You know him. He was Sheriff DeWitt's deputy."

"I will mention him to Judge Morrow, but because he is on active duty and stationed out west, I don't think he would be approved. It would be too hard for him to meet some of his obligations. But I will mention him."

"When will you see the judge?"

"Not until next week, I will have to make an appointment with him. In the meantime, I can start to evaluate your mother's estate. I will have to do that, no matter who is going to be the executor."

"What will you do?"

"I will need to find out about all of her bank accounts, other assets, and debts. And, I will have to appraise the house and any other property."

As Tilley mentioned the house, Connie stood in front of her chair. She did not speak but kept her eyes on Tilley's.

As he finished his sentence, he noticed Connie standing. He started to stand too, but settled into his chair. He looked at her and turned away.

"Hasn't the house been appraised for taxes?" Elizabeth asked. "We just paid them and there was a value for the house listed."

With a sigh, he said, "Tax value and estate value are different. It is too complicated."

Standing Elizabeth said, "Then I must find someone who understands so they can explain the difference to me. Mr. Tilley, are there any obligations to be paid immediately?"

"Uh, uh, no. Nothing I know of."

"Nor do I. It is time for us to go, and Mr. Tilley, if we must have an executor and a guardian, we prefer he conduct all the business of the estate. We will wait until Judge Morrow appoints someone. Good day."

Still seated, Tilley mumbled, "But, I..." as Elizabeth and Connie started out.

As they opened the door, Virginia turned from the filing cabinet next to the frosted glass wall that separated her office from Mr. Tilley's. With a pleasant smile she said, "Good afternoon, ladies, if I can help you with anything, please call."

Connie turned to her and smiled, "Thank you, Miss Virginia, thank you very much."

Neither Elizabeth nor Connie spoke until they were in the car. "He's the one, Betty May. Mr. Tilley wants our house, or something in it. And, Betty May, he knows the man who shot my Momma."

"Damn it, John. Elizabeth DuBose is as big a bitch as her mother ever was. And the little one is as creepy as hell. Half the time they were in my office she stood there and stared at me. It was like she was trying to read my mind."

"I can see you were your usual charming self, Hiram."

"Hell, I tried, but with the little girl there, shit..." Tilley's voice trailed. He added, "They know something though. They know about the money. No doubt about that."

"Calm down, Hiram. We will work slow, like we planned. When are you going to see Judge Morrow?"

"As soon as I can next week, but it will likely be Tuesday."

"Remember, Morrow and Jefferson DuBose were friends, and you are looking out for the best interest of the girls."

"I've got no damn interest in the girls, just our money."

Elizabeth and Connie didn't start for Athens until about ten o'clock. At the end of the drive, they waited as Sheriff DeWitt drove out toward Godfrey's store in his black Ford. He slowed and waved but didn't stop. "Let's stop by and see Diane," Elizabeth said.

When they got out at the sheriff's office, they saw Virginia from Mr. Tilley's office walking toward the court house.

"Oh, Elizabeth and Connie, I am glad you stopped in. I wanted to see you," Diane said.

"Is something the matter? We saw the sheriff going out our road," Elizabeth answered.

"No, nothing out your way. But you two set Hiram Tilley on fire yesterday."

"Why? How? We were nice and listened to what he said."

"I didn't like him," Connie said.

"Well, Connie, he didn't like your sister telling him 'no'. Mr. Tilley doesn't like to be told 'no', and especially not by a woman. Virginia said he cussed for five minutes and went storming out, probably to see John Harwell."

"I told him we would wait until the judge appointed someone before we talked about mother's business. I wonder how quick it will be? I wish Bill were here."

"Virginia said she was going to call Judge Morrow and get Mr. Tilley an appointment as soon as she could next week," Diane said. "I'll call my friend Mary and see how Judge Morrow's schedule is next week. Maybe he is going to be busy until Thursday or Friday."

"I don't understand," Elizabeth said.

"You will if you get a job in a man's world. Like in the court house, it is the men who get elected, but it is the women who make things happen. And sometimes, we don't make things happen."

Connie walked to Diane and said, "I like you, Diane. You are smart."

"I'm still not sure I understand," Elizabeth said.

"Don't worry, Betty May. I will explain it to you on the way to Athens."

"Mr. Tilley," Virginia said, "Judge Morrow has a busy schedule next week. He can see you late on Friday or most any time on Monday or Tuesday."

"Damn, is that the best you could do?"

"I'll get Mary on the phone if you want to talk to her."

"Hell no. Shit, Friday is no better than Monday. Tell her ten o'clock on Monday," as he slammed the door to his office.

With a smile, Virginia said, "Yes sir," to no one. After a moment on the telephone, she knocked at the door. "Mary says something has come up and she has you down for eleven on Monday."

Elizabeth carried her packages to her room, and Connie dropped hers in the parlor and went to the bathroom under the front stairs. As she came out the telephone rang. She answered and called to Elizabeth, "It's Bill. Hurry. He says he doesn't have much time."

"Oh, Bill, I have so much to tell you," she said. After a very short pause, she spoke a disappointed, "Okay." and was quiet listening for a few minutes. "I understand and I love you too. I miss you so. Goodbye."

Connie looked at her sister, "What's the matter, Betty May?"

"Nothing really. He is starting for Boston and didn't have time to talk. He told me to listen to him." Everybody tells me what to do. No, every man tells me what to do. "But, Connie, he might get home next week."

Elizabeth and Connie spent Saturday and Sunday deciding on and packing clothes and a few of their things to move to Athens. Sunday night Bill called from Boston. He said he was really in Cambridge and it was snowing and cold, and he was in a hotel. "Tomorrow, I will go to the school and see about classes, and maybe look for an apartment."

Elizabeth listened. She could tell he was excited. When he finished, she told him about the meeting with Mr. Tilley, and how Connie thought he wanted their house.

Bill said, "I'll go talk to Judge Morrow for you when I get home and ask him about all of this."

"I'll go with you," Elizabeth responded.

"I guess that will be okay. He asked about you and Connie when I met him last month."

Elizabeth hung up with an "I love you." As she walked to the kitchen, Bill's "I guess that will be okay," caught in her throat and stayed. *It is my damn house.*

Monday morning, Diane called to tell Elizabeth Mr. Tilley couldn't see Judge Morrow until the next Monday. Maybe sometimes women did make things happen or not happen.

Tuesday, Clara came to clean and Elizabeth and Connie drove into Greensboro. They got their mail, looked at Christmas tree decorations at the Big Store, and ate dinner at Geer's. At their drive, they met Travis and Clara heading home. Elizabeth looked around the clean kitchen and decided on a light supper and not messing up Clara's work.

At four, the phone rang, and Connie answered. "Betty May, it's Bill."

"Elizabeth, I got done today and I'm coming home tomorrow. Can you meet me at Bush Field?"

"Yes, of course. What time? That's wonderful. How?"

"I don't know exactly what time, but it will be late afternoon. Drive on the base and ask directions to the air field. Be sure to tell them you are to meet Major Brown's flight. They will help you. It's all Army flights, and there is no real schedule."

"We will be there," Elizabeth answered.

"Got to go. Tomorrow."

Connie was excited too. "I might wear one of my new school dresses tomorrow. I want to look nice. That'd be okay wouldn't it, Betty May?"

"Yes," she replied. "I want to look nice too." She pushed open the door to her mother's room. Less than a year ago, it was her mother's and father's room. Now the closets and drawers were empty, the room was clean, and her parent's bed was freshly made. The curtains were pulled closed on the big bay window. In the waning light, the room was dark. She pushed the curtains open and turned on the table lamp by the bed. "That's better." She walked to Connie's room.

"What about this one, Betty May?" Connie said as she held one of her new dresses.

"I like it," Elizabeth answered. "What would you think about me moving into mother's and daddy's bedroom?"

"You mean, you are going to sleep in there?"

"Yes, and put my clothes in there too."

"Okay," Connie said as she started to consider another outfit.

Elizabeth looked around the only bedroom she remembered. There wasn't much in the room, the little bed, an end table with a lamp, a chest, and the dressing table she made by tacking a skirt of pretty print around three sides of a small kitchen table. No, the little bed wouldn't do.

She took the top drawer from her chest into her mother's room and transferred the contents to her mother's chest and returned for the second. Working on the third drawer, she found another envelope with $300 in it tacked to the back drawer. *We better check in Connie's room too.*

She looked at the little dressing table. *This is Betty May's table and Betty May's things. They belong to the little girl who lived in here. I'll not move them. In the morning, I'll move my clothes into my room.*

10

Elizabeth slept well in the bigger bed. After coffee and a cold cereal breakfast, she moved her clothes to her new room and closed the door to her old one.

Connie changed clothes twice before they left. "How long will it take to get to Bill's airplane?" Connie asked.

"Bush Field is near Augusta. It will take us about an hour and a half to drive there. We can stop in Harlem and get something to eat. Bill didn't know when he would get there, so we might have to wait."

The only thing to identify where they should wait was a low building with a tower rising from its flat roof. It was separated from the tarmac airstrip by a high chain-link fence.

"Is this the place, Betty May? It doesn't look like there's any place to sit. And, I have to go to the bathroom."

Elizabeth parked the Packard by a pickup truck painted olive-drab. "I'll go and ask inside."

"I'm coming with you," Connie said as she got out and started toward the building.

Inside a surprised sergeant looked as Connie asked, "Where's the bathroom?"

"Ma'am, it is outside on the back. It is the only door."

Without comment, Connie turned and walked out the door. Elizabeth said, "Sir."

"Sergeant, ma'am. I'm Sergeant Bookert. May I help you?"

Elizabeth explained, and Sergeant Bookert looked at a clip board and ran a pencil down the page held there. "We have a transport due in about 1600 hours," he said. "It is coming from Phillips in Maryland. He could be on that."

"That's four o'clock?"

"Yes ma'am. The plane should be on the way now. Who did you say you are waiting for?"

"Bill Brown, Major William Brown. He is on special assignment at MIT in Boston."

Sergeant Bookert sat up and said, "Yes ma'am. Major Brown. I'll call Phillips right now and see if he is on the flight."

"Thank you, sergeant," Elizabeth said as Connie returned.

"You need to clean your bathroom," she said. "And there were no towels to wash your hands."

"Yes ma'am," Bookert answered as he took the telephone. "This is Bookert at the tower, get me the tower at Phillips in Maryland." A short pause, "No, I'll talk to anyone there."

Elizabeth and Connie heard him mention Bill's name and rank twice. "Ma'am, Major Brown is on the transport and their eta is 1550, uh, estimated time of arrival is ten minutes until four. In about an hour."

Connie and Elizabeth waited in the car. At quarter 'til four, Connie saw Sergeant Bookert climb a ladder to the tower above his building. In a few minutes an airplane appeared as a small green dot. They watched it land and taxi to the far side of the field. Bookert came down from the tower, waved to them and gave a thumbs up. Fifteen minutes later, a jeep sped across the tarmac to the gate in front of them. Bill got out, returned a salute to the jeep driver and grabbed his bag.

Bill said, "Elizabeth May DuBose, I've missed you and I am ready to go home. And you, Connie, I've missed you too."

"Bill," Connie said, "you look different."

"Yes, you do," Elizabeth agreed. "You have some color."

"I guess two weeks in the New Mexico sunshine did that. I know I've lost a little weight. Those Geer's Cafe breakfasts didn't help my pants size. But I might be ready for one while I'm home."

It was nearly seven when they reached the house. During the drive, Bill talked about everything he had done over the past three weeks. He was excited and pleased. Elizabeth listened almost without comment.

Clara had come over in the afternoon and fixed supper. It was in the oven. They ate quietly. The long day wore on all of them. After Elizabeth and Connie cleared the table, Elizabeth suggested Connie might go to her room. She didn't argue.

In the parlor, Connie kissed Bill on the cheek. "Good night," she said, "We can talk more tomorrow."

Elizabeth went upstairs with Connie. When she came down, she said, "Bill, I have a lot to tell you, and there is a lot for us to talk about. But first, I am going to fix me a whiskey. Would you like one?"

"You? Whiskey? I am surprised, and yes, I would like one."

"Whiskey because we are out of wine. That's one of the things I want to talk about," Elizabeth answered.

Elizabeth went over everything that had happened. The more she talked the angrier she got. After a few minutes, Bill said, "Darling, I think…"

Elizabeth cut him off, "Don't say anything right now, Bill. I am not finished."

After another twenty minutes, Elizabeth said, "So I am damned tired of men telling me what I can and can't do, and I must have their permission before I can take care of my family."

"Elizabeth," Bill started.

"And, that goes for you too, Bill Brown. Tonight, and in my house, I am in charge. Wait here." Elizabeth finished her whiskey in one swallow and made a face.

Bill sat quietly.

In a moment, Elizabeth came down the front stairs and into the parlor. She was wearing a robe and had a small box in her hand. Standing in front of him, she handed him the box. It was the condoms she and Connie found in her father's desk. "Do you know what these are?"

"Yes, of course." Rethinking his answer, he added, "Army hygiene training."

"Good," Elizabeth answered. "My room is now the one above the parlor. Take these and go wait for me. I'll be a few minutes."

11

Elizabeth pushed on Bill's bare shoulder. "Wake my love. We have to go to Crawfordville this morning and see Judge Morrow."

As Bill turned to her, he asked, "What time is it?"

"It's five." She put her arms around him.

At six, she said, "I hear Connie. I am going to get out of bed now, take a bath and start breakfast. You bathe and get dressed. Wear your uniform."

"Yes, ma'am."

At the table, Bill asked, "How did you get an appointment to see Judge Morrow?"

"Diane, she said it was something she did."

"Connie, I think you should wait here in Mary's office while Bill and I talk to Judge Morrow."

"Okay, Betty May. But I would like to say hello to him. Momma said he was daddy's friend."

Judge Morrow opened the door to his office. "Come in and sit down. Bill, I want to catch up."

After speaking to Connie, the judge followed Elizabeth and

Bill into his office. Elizabeth explained all that had happened since her father died, and what she had done since her mother's funeral. She ended with, "Do I have to have someone to do the things I've been doing? And, if I do, why can't it be Bill. We are going to get married."

"Elizabeth, the law is clear on this. Since you are not twenty-one, there must be an executor for your mother's estate who is twenty-one, and Connie must have a legal guardian."

"I understand. Can it be Bill?"

"If Bill were still living here, I would have no problem appointing him; or if you were married, I would appoint him. But given the current situation, I can't appoint Bill. I'm sorry."

"Judge Morrow," Bill asked, "are you saying if we were married right now, you would appoint me to be Connie's guardian and executor of Mary Greene's estate?"

"That's right. You would have cause to question anyone else I appointed as executor," Judge Morrow answered.

"That's the answer," Bill said as reached and took Elizabeth's hand. "We will get married right now. You can marry us can't you, Judge Morrow?"

"Yes, I can," the judge replied. "But marriage is a big step, you need to be sure. Do you have a license?"

"No, but can't we get one here?"

"Yes, but you have to wait twenty-four hours to marry. And, I'm leaving tonight for a long weekend in Atlanta, and I won't be here until Monday.

"If we have a license, any preacher can marry us, right?" Elizabeth asked.

"Yes, after twenty-four hours."

Elizabeth turned to Bill and said, "Bill Brown, will you marry me?"

"Yes, I will, and I will pay for the license."

Judge Morrow stood, "I will have Mary prepare the papers appointing Bill executor and guardian. They will be ready to sign on Monday. Bring me your signed license on Monday and I will make the appointments official."

"Thank you, Judge Morrow," Elizabeth said. "I know why my daddy said he liked you. Thank you so much."

Connie sat quietly in the outer office and watched Mary as she typed. *How does she know where to put her fingers?* The bell on the typewriter dinged and Mary's hand swatted the silver handle.

A lady came to the door and said quietly, "Mrs. Watkins."

"Hello, Mrs. de Graffinreed. Judge Morrow has someone with him right now, but they should be done in a few minutes. Please have a seat."

At the sound of the name, Connie moaned, "Oh," and pulled her legs to her chest.

The two ladies looked at Connie. "Are you all right?" Mary asked.

With her eyes tightly closed, Connie shook her head, "Yes," but she didn't look well.

All turned toward the door to Judge Morrow's office as it opened. Connie opened her eyes and darted between Mary's desk and Mrs. de Graffinreed to her sister.

"I don't know what, but something must have scared her," Mary said. "I was typing and when Mrs...."

As soon as he saw Mrs. de Graffinreed, Judge Morrow never let Mary finish. He remembered the bad blood between Mrs. de Graffinreed's husband and Elizabeth and Connie's father. "Good morning," he said to Mrs. de Graffinreed. "Please come in and have a seat. I will be right with you," as he escorted her into his office and returned to the outer office, closing the door behind him.

Connie had started to cry. Sniffling softly, she pulled at Elizabeth to leave.

"Mary," Judge Morrow said, "Please take Bill and Elizabeth down to Inez. They need a marriage license. Bring the county copy with you. We'll need the information for me to write orders."

"Yes sir," Mary replied. "Congratulations, Bill and Elizabeth. When is the wedding?"

As they started down the hall, Bill said, "We have to work that out, but it will be before Monday. I think we want to keep it a secret until we are married."

"I understand," Mary said.

Connie calmed some as soon as they were out of the office. At the top of the stairs, Elizabeth waited and leaned down to Connie. "I know you have something important to tell me, but can it wait a few minutes? I have important news too."

Connie said, "Yes. Mine is about Momma."

With their marriage license in hand, Elizabeth and Bill walked out of the court house with Connie a step ahead. At the sidewalk, Connie turned and said, "Betty May, Miss Mary called the lady who came in Mrs. de Graffinreed. That's the name of the man who killed Momma!"

"How do you know that?" Bill asked. "Are you sure?"

"You know how Connie knows things. She said all along, the man who killed Momma had a funny name, and she would know it if she heard it."

"I understand about Connie knowing, but when I came to see Judge Morrow about the Annie Mattox murder, I found out the depot agent here is a man named Hans de Graffinreed," Bill said.

"Hans is his name," Connie added, "Hans de Graffinreed killed my Momma! But he is dead now."

Bill looked at Connie, "I'll talk to Sheriff DeWitt next week and I'll find out what I can about de Graffinreed. Is that okay?"

"Yes, Bill, but he is dead," Connie answered.

"Connie, I asked Bill to marry me and he said 'yes'. We are going to get married before Monday. What do you think?"

"I think you act like you are married already. Will Bill be my step-father?"

"No, I will be your brother-in-law."

"And he will be your legal guardian," Elizabeth added.

"Okay. Where are you going to get married?"

"We don't know yet. We have to find a preacher," Elizabeth said.

"Let's go to Greensboro and start looking," Bill said.

"We can go this afternoon," Elizabeth replied. "Moses is coming to the house to get paid, then we can look."

As Bill got into the Packard, he said, "We'll call Diane and tell her. Maybe she'll have an idea."

"Oh, I am sure Diane knows by now, but she will have an idea," Elizabeth said with a smile.

On the ride home, they named all the preachers they knew,

and none seemed like a good choice. Bill remembered Hiram Tilley could perform a marriage, but both Elizabeth and Connie rejected him immediately.

"Bill, we do want to keep this a secret until we marry. I wouldn't want Tilley to do something to stop us."

"It won't be a secret long if you go to asking preachers in Greensboro," Connie said.

"You are right, Connie. I could call my mother in Sandy Springs and go there. Besides, I do need to tell my mother and sister we are getting married."

"That is a good idea," Elizabeth said. "Other than Diane and Sheriff DeWitt, there is nobody here I would care about coming to our wedding."

"It might have been a good idea. But I just remembered they all were going to Chattanooga to visit Robbie's parents."

As they turned in the drive, they saw a wagon in the distance. "That's probably Moses," Elizabeth said. "He and Travis fixed the fence and a few other things, Clara has been cleaning, and taking washing to Liza. They have been a big help."

Moses stopped his wagon, and Bill, Elizabeth, and Connie went out. Moses pointed to two older children in the bed of the wagon, "These Corina's grands. Clara be watching them while Travis and Tom are up to the church decorating for Christmas. Angel, Harrison, make your manners."

The girl stood in the wagon and said, "Good morning, Miss Elizabeth, Miss Cornelia, and sir." Harrison stood and mumbled as Angel spoke.

Elizabeth and Bill nodded. Elizabeth said, "Moses, Clara, come in the kitchen and let's take care of our business."

"Yes, ma'am."

Clara gave her baby to Angel.

Connie stayed out as the four adults went into the house. Looking at Angel, she thought she recognized the coat she was wearing as Elizabeth's. "She lets you hold the baby? How old are you?" Connie asked.

"I'm ten, and I take care of babies all the time. These is my cousins, Travis and Clara's little girl, Annie and this baby is Elyse."

"I'm ten too. Can I hold Elyse?"

"Not on the ground. If you climb in the wagon, I'll let you hold her."

Connie sat crossed legged in the bed of the wagon with baby Elyse in her arms. With her dark eyes wide open, Elyse looked at this stranger holding her.

"She's smiling at you," Angel said. "She likes you."

"I like her too," Connie said and kissed the baby on the top of her head. She laughed and said, "Her hair feels funny."

Angel reached out and touched Connie's straight, light brown hair and said, "I 'spect your hair'd feel funny to her."

"My sister and Bill have to get married before Monday, and they can't find a preacher. We are going to try and find one this afternoon," Connie said.

"Is she going to have a baby?" Angel asked.

"Why did you ask that?" Connie said.

"Most times when there is a wedding in a hurry a baby comes soon after. My big sister, Mavis, got married and she already had a big baby belly."

Connie said, "I don't think there's a baby. It is about the law and who is going to guard me. Betty May wants Bill to guard me, and Mr. Tilley wants somebody else. I want Bill too. But I think they have to be married for it to be Bill."

Moses and Clara came from the house. "I better give Elyse to you," Connie said. She jumped from the wagon and waved, "It was nice to talk to you, Angel, come to see me. Bye Mr. Moses, Miss Clara."

Elizabeth was fixing sandwiches for dinner and Bill was trying to call his sister's home even though he thought they weren't there.

Bill walked into the kitchen from the parlor and said, "Moses is coming back, and the operator didn't get an answer. I'm sure they've gone to Chattanooga. Wonder what Moses wants?" Bill walked out to meet the wagon.

Bill and Moses talked a minute. Bill called, "Elizabeth, please come out."

"Moses, please ask Miss Elizabeth. This will be for her to decide."

"Miss Elizabeth, your family has been good to us, and all we want to do is help. Angel says Miss Cornelia says you can't find a preacher to marry you before Monday. Our Reverend Manigault will do it at our church or at your house whenever you say."

"Moses that is very kind of you, but..."

Bill interrupted, "Think about this a minute. We don't want people to know right away, and we don't have anybody who will come, except maybe Diane and the sheriff. Why not?"

Excited, Clara said, "Miss Elizabeth, our church always looks real nice for Christmas. Everybody knows how kind you been to us."

Connie looked at Moses, "Mr. Moses, can you play your horn for the wedding like you did for Momma's funeral?"

"Yes, ma'am, Miss Cornelia. I'd be pleased, and we could have some other music too, a lot of music."

"Say yes, Betty May. Let's get married in Mr. Moses' church on Sunday. Please!"

Turning to Bill, Elizabeth said, "I guess it makes sense, and nobody in town will find out until we are ready. Yes, Connie we will get married on Sunday. Thank you, Moses."

Moses smiled and said, "Yes'm. We'll take care of everything. Would three o'clock be a good time?"

Bill looked at Elizabeth. She said, "Three o'clock is fine."

"Yes'm."

A smiling Clara touched her father-in-law's arm, "Mr. Jackson, we need to hurry home. There's a lot to do to get ready."

As he turned the wagon, Moses said, "We do. I'll stop at Corina's and tell her to spread the word and go to the church to tell Reverend Manigault. I hope the sheriff do come."

12

As he sat down to eat, Bill said, "This has been quite a morning, but now everything's all worked out, I can see an afternoon nap in my future."

"Say a blessing, Bill," Elizabeth said as she extended her hands to him and Connie. When he finished, Elizabeth held on to his hand, "I am getting married on Sunday. You too. Everything is not 'worked out'. I don't have a dress. What are you going to wear? What will Connie wear?"

Five minutes later Elizabeth caught her breath and Bill said, "Oh." In another five, he said, "We'll go to Athens first thing in the morning. I'll call Mr. Breeden at Gallant-Belk right now about a suit."

"You might need a suit, but I want you in your dress uniform. You didn't take it to Alamogordo." Elizabeth called after him as he walked to the phone, "First, call Sheriff DeWitt and ask him to come, you need a best man. And, I want to talk with Diane."

"Diane's coming and she's going to bring Pete. Ben and Gwen

are coming too. He will stand with me. Diane gave me Mr. Breeden's number. I'll call right now. Then what?"

"I'll let you know 'what' when I know." *I need to make a list so I can keep things straight. Where's my tablet? Something old, something new, something borrowed, something blue. I'll get 'new' tomorrow.*

Elizabeth worked on her list, but Bill got no new assignments. Mostly he watched Elizabeth. "Do something, Bill," she said.

"Okay. When was the last time you had the oil changed in the Packard?"

"Not since Daddy died, but we haven't driven much."

"I'll be a little while. Maybe I can get it washed too."

When he returned, both Elizabeth and Connie were asleep in their chairs in the parlor. He took the big bed upstairs.

After supper, Elizabeth said, "I've made my list and already checked off a few things. What about you?"

"Jack Breeden said he had the right suit for me and he's having it altered now. It should be ready by noon tomorrow. He's throwing in a shirt and tie for a wedding present."

"Good, I can cross one thing off."

"Connie, turn on the radio and find H. V. Kaltenborn. I want to hear what he has to say about China. I think the *Aldrich Family* comes on after.

"Hen-*reeeeeeeeeeee!* Hen-ree *Al*-drich!" came from the speaker of the big Philco radio, and Connie was lost to the room.

"Well, there is one more thing," Bill said as he walked to the back stairs. When he returned, he knelt on one knee in front of Elizabeth. Connie never turned from the radio.

"I planned to save this until Christmas, but since we are getting married ten days before, I think this is a good time." He held a small black box with 'EB Horn' in gold on top. He opened the box and moved it to Elizabeth.

"What?"

"It's an engagement ring. I know it is not a big diamond, but the green stone looks good with your red hair. It is a sapphire."

"Oh, Bill, I love it. It is perfect."

The conversation caught Connie's attention. "Let me see," she said as Bill slipped the ring on Elizabeth's finger.

"It's pretty. Don't you like it, Betty May?"

"Yes. Where's my list? I've forgotten rings. We need wedding rings, silver ones to match my engagement ring."

"Platinum," Bill said.

13

Sunday morning, Connie came down the front stairs to the bathroom. After, she found Elizabeth in the kitchen. "Betty May, Bill's taking a bath."

"When he's finished, you take your bath. I took mine early. We have a busy day."

"I know. Betty May why did Bill sleep in the front room the last two nights when he'd been sleeping with you?"

Elizabeth laughed, "Connie, there sure is a lot in that question. Right now, I don't have a good answer, except today is our wedding day, and from now on, we will sleep in the same bed."

As Bill turned the Packard down the path to Little Zion Church, he asked, "Did you imagine your wedding would be like this?"

"At school, most of the girls talked all about their wedding plans, even if they didn't have a boyfriend. Since I had never been to a wedding, I didn't understand why all the fuss."

"You were in college and had never been to a wedding?"

"Nope, no weddings, no funerals, and only a few times to church with Daddy."

"Your mother talked about the Bible all the time. I'm surprised."

"Momma had her own ideas about everything, and mostly she talked about Saint Paul. When my roommate found out I'd never been to a funeral, she and some other girls took me to one in town. Nobody knew the lady who died. They said I needed the experience, and you didn't need an invitation to a funeral. We dressed up and walked to the church."

Connie said, "Momma's and Daddy's funerals are the only one I've been to, and I haven't been to a wedding either."

"The summer after my first year at GSCW, I went to two weddings of girls I knew in school. Both of them were quickly planned, if you know what I mean."

"I'll bet those girls were going to have a baby soon," Connie said.

"Connie! I'm not going to have a baby anytime soon."

Changing the subject, Bill asked, "Connie, do you know what a honeymoon is?"

"No. And that's a funny thing to say, honeymoon."

"It's a trip a bride and groom take right after the wedding, like a short vacation," Bill explained.

"We won't have one," Elizabeth said. "Going to see Judge Morrow in Crawfordville doesn't count. But seeing him is important."

"Yes," agreed Bill, "but maybe we can get away for a day or two right after Christmas."

"Where would we go?" Connie asked.

Elizabeth started to answer, when Bill interrupted. "Later, Elizabeth. There's Ben and Gwen. He's here early and politicking."

"And, there's Diane and Pete. Good."

"What's that?" Connie asked as she pointed toward the front of the church.

"It's a manger scene," Elizabeth answered. "They've made a stable out of cedar posts, and there's the manger. I bet the children play the parts on Christmas Eve."

"Manger?"

"You remember. Daddy used to read us the story from the Bible on Christmas Eve. Mary had the baby Jesus in a stable and put him in a manger, a feed trough for cows."

"I remember, and the shepherds came to see him. Miss Clara said the church would be fixed nice, and it is. I like the big wreath and red bow on the door. Betty May can we have one?"

"Yes," Elizabeth answered. Turning to Bill she said, "Momma thought Christmas trees and all the decorations weren't right for Jesus' birthday, so we never had them. I told Connie we would have a tree this year. You'll help, won't you?"

Bill took Elizabeth's hand and looked at Connie, "Elizabeth, Connie, our first Christmas as a family will be special. We will have a wreath on the door and a tree. Maybe a big tree with lots of lights. Now, come on. Let's go get married."

Liza, Clara, and Angel appeared. "Mr. Bill," Liza said, "you do look good in your uniform, but you and Sheriff DeWitt need to go in the church with Reverend Manigault and wait. Now go on. We've got bride things to do."

"Good afternoon, Gwen, Ben. Thank you for coming. Ben,

they said you and I needed to go in," Bill said as he walked to his former boss.

"Hello, Bill. It is good to see you again," Gwen said. "You and Ben go on. I'll come in with Diane and Pete."

Little Zion Church was one room. It looked smaller from the inside. Jacob Manigault stood in front of a small table that served as the altar.

"Come in, gentlemen," he said and walked to meet the two white men. "Sheriff DeWitt, it is an honor to have you here today, and Major Brown we are pleased we can be of service to you and Miss Elizabeth."

"Thank you for offering to help," Bill said.

Moses came in from the side door near them. He had his trumpet.

"Jacob, when this gets out, you might get some grief for doing this," the sheriff said.

"Miss DuBose has been kind to us, and some trouble is always in the air. We'll get along," Reverend Manigault answered.

"Elizabeth and I don't want any trouble for y'all," Bill said. "Maybe we better go."

"Won't matter iffen you do," Moses said. "They'll say we was getting above our place just to ask. We'll get along like Reverend Manigault say. Now we gots to get you two married."

The front door opened, and two more men came in, one with a violin case and the other with a guitar.

"I need to see to the music," Moses said. He joined the others in the front corner. "Brother Isley, you take the lead on 'Faithfulness' when folks is coming in. I'll bring her down the aisle with 'Love Devine'.

Four ladies, dressed in white, put white bows on the chairs at the end of each row and neatly lined them to make an aisle. From a cupboard near the door, two of them took candles and set them on the sills of the glassless windows. As the candles were set and lit, the shutters were closed from the outside. The other two ladies lit the candles on the altar. All four left and closed the doors. Sunlight leaked through the shutters and around doors. The candlelight softened it to a warm golden glow that seemed to flow from the candles on the altar. Reverend Manigault led Bill and Ben to their places, and the church was silent.

Moses looked at the man with the guitar and nodded. He strummed the opening chord of *Great is Thy Faithfulness*, Brother Isley raised his bow and started the melody. As soon as the music started, the front door opened, and Gwen DeWitt came in on the arm of a young man who looked to be about sixteen. They walked to the front between the rows of chairs. The young man released Gwen's arm and gestured the first chair on the right side of the church. Gwen turned to the left, spoke quietly to the young man and took the first chair. Diane came in next on the arm of another young man. Pete followed. They sat beside Gwen.

The church filled quickly, and the doors were closed. Moses nodded, and the musicians finished the verse. Moses brought his horn to his lips and played a fanfare. The doors opened and Angel started down the aisle. She had a few rose petals in a small basket, and she dropped them by ones and twos as she walked toward Reverend Manigault. At the front, she turned and stood by Sheriff DeWitt.

The church became quiet as the notes of the trumpet faded.

Moses started *Love Devine, All Loves Excelling*, and Connie appeared in the door.

Bill looked. *She's changed clothes! That's a pretty dress.*"

At the chorus, the other musicians joined in, and Reverend Manigault stepped forward and lifted his hands for all to stand.

Elizabeth stepped into the open door, and Bill looked at his bride. "Oh!" he said.

Ben DeWitt put his hand on Bill's shoulder with a little squeeze.

Riding over, Elizabeth had been in a cream-colored wool suit with a matching hat. She said the suit was okay for an informal day-time wedding. Now she was in a wedding dress, a real wedding dress with a lacy veil. Her auburn hair was down, not pinned under the small hat she had worn over.

Bill smiled.

Ben leaned to Bill's ear, "You didn't know, did you?"

He shook his head, "No".

"Diane and Gwen helped cook this up."

Connie reached the front, smiled at Bill and tried to wink, turned to the left and faced the congregation.

Bill never took his eyes from Elizabeth. Two steps away, she mouthed, "Surprise," and Bill nodded, "Yes." She took his extended hand, gave her bouquet to Connie, and they turned to face Reverend Manigault who seated the congregation with a gesture.

"Brothers and Sisters, we are gathered here today..."

14

Bill woke to an empty bed, a disappointment, but the aroma of coffee and bacon pleased him. He called from the top of the back-stairs, "Mrs. Brown, Mr. Brown is going to take a bath and dress."

"Yes, Mr. Brown," Elizabeth called back.

Bill walked into the kitchen in the same uniform he had worn for the flight to Bush. He kissed his new bride and took the cup of coffee she held out. "I need some clothes," he said. Some civies to leave here and for Cambridge. I don't have to wear a uniform at school."

"We can go to Athens after we see Judge Morrow," Elizabeth answered. "And, you need to sign some papers for me and Connie there, Mr. Brown, Mr. Guardian, Mr. Executor."

"Connie's out of bed," Elizabeth said as they heard the upstairs toilet flush. "We'll be ready to eat in a few minutes."

"Okay," Bill said as he turned to the parlor, "I want to look at..." and his voice trailed off as he got into the hall way.

"Are we going on the honey thing today?" Connie asked as she came into the kitchen from the backstairs.

"It's a honeymoon," Bill answered as he came in from the parlor. "And, it is only for the bride and groom."

Connie frowned.

"Don't worry, Connie. You'll have something special to do if we can have a honeymoon. But today we are going to Crawford-ville and to Athens," Elizabeth said.

"Why are we going to Athens?" Connie asked, clearly not interested.

Bill said, "Elizabeth says I have some business, but after we can shop for decorations and a wreath for our front door."

"That's good, Bill. Do I have to call you anything else since you are guarding me? Angel said her momma made the wreath at the church."

Bill smiled. "I like Bill, but not Billy and especially not Billy Boy. That was a pretty wreath at the church. We'll see about getting her to make us one for our front door."

At Judge Morrow's office, Mary wanted to hear all about the wedding.

"It was at Moses' church near our house," Connie answered. "It was all decorated for Christmas with a manger and wreaths."

"Moses' church?" Mary asked. "Who is he?"

"He's our friend," Connie continued the conversation. "He helps us sometimes and Clara and Liza clean our house."

Elizabeth handed Mary their signed marriage license. "I think everything is signed."

"Little Zion Church, Reverend Jacob Mani, Mana...," Mary read, stumbling on the minister's name.

"He says Man-a-go," Bill said, sounding out the name.

Mary stood, "Let me take these in to Judge Morrow. He has

the other papers with him." Mary closed the door behind her. "Judge Morrow, I think they were married in a colored church! Does it count?"

The judge took the offered license from Mary and read. Looking he said, "I know Jacob Manigault. He is a good man and loves the Lord. They are as married as good as if the ceremony had been in First Baptist in Atlanta. Please send in the newlyweds."

"Congratulations and best wishes to all three of you. When I sign these other papers, you will be one family. Have a seat," Judge Morrow said. "Getting married yesterday and not in town, I don't guess many know of this yet."

"No, sir," Bill answered. "Ben, Gwen, Diane, and her friend Pete were the only ones from town." We asked them not to say anything until we had all the papers signed."

Judge Morrow signed, shuffled four pages together and extended them toward Bill. Elizabeth leaned forward and took them and looked at the top page. "Elizabeth," he said, "you have two copies of the order naming William M. Brown as executor of your mother's estate and two copies of an order naming the same William M. Brown as Cornelia's legal guardian. Give one of each to Virginia at the court house. The other copy is for you and Bill."

Elizabeth smiled, "Thank you so much, Judge Morrow. Getting this done is such a relief for me."

"I hope that's not the only reason you married."

Bill took Elizabeth's hand and said, "No sir, Judge Morrow. We love each other."

"They do," Connie added. "They kiss and hug all the time."

"Good," and Judge Morrow continued, "Connie when you were here last week, did the lady who came in upset you? Her name was Mrs. de Graffinreed."

"When I heard her name, I knew de Graffinreed is the name of the man who shot my momma."

"How do you know that?"

"I just know. I didn't know the name until I heard it, but that's who shot my momma. I think he's dead now. My momma may have shot him in the head."

"Mrs. de Graffinreed didn't know your mother or anything about her husband shooting anybody. She is sad her husband is dead. If she knew, I'm sure she would be sad to know about your mother."

"Can I say a prayer?"

"Certainly," the judge answered.

Connie bowed her head and was quiet for a moment, she spoke of peace for de Graffinreed and her mother.

When she raised her head, Judge Morrow said, "Thank you, Connie. I believe we've finished many things today." He stood, "Merry Christmas to the new Brown family."

The three stood on the steps of the Taliaferro County Court House. "I'm glad this part is over," Elizabeth said. "Let's get to Athens. We'll take these papers to Greensboro in the morning."

Hiram Tilley stepped around the corner and stopped short at the sight of the trio coming from the courthouse. Surprised, he called out, "Miss DuBose, Miss DuBose, I want to talk with you. Wait."

Connie turned and walked toward him, the others followed. Looking at Mr. Tilley, Connie said, "What do you want?"

"I want to speak to the other Miss DuBose, your sister," Tilley answered.

"I'm the only Miss DuBose here," Connie said. Turning to her sister, she continued, "She's Mrs. Brown, and Mr. Brown is my guard."

Elizabeth joined her sister and Bill stood behind watching with some enjoyment. Elizabeth said, "Yes, Mr. Tilley, Bill and I were married on Sunday at Little Zion Church, and this morning, Judge Morrow appointed Bill as executor of mother's estate and as Connie's legal guardian. We'll bring the papers in tomorrow morning. Perhaps if I have time, we can talk more. Good Day. Let's go, Bill, we have much to do."

Standing alone on the sidewalk, Tilley mumbled, "Little Zion, Little Zion."

"Damn it, John. It's the little one who screws things up. It's like she knows what we want. I'll bet she knows where the money is. I'll bet I could get her to tell me. I could scare her."

"Calm down, Hiram. We've got time. Remember Brown is now in the Army and he's not going to be around. We'll figure something out."

"I'm damned tired of waiting. And with DuBose and de Graffinreed gone, that's twice the money for us."

15

"My beautiful bride, I have a request of you."

"Yes, Mr. Brown."

Connie looked at the two sitting across from her at the little yellow table in the kitchen, "Y'all are sure silly sometimes."

"Mrs. Brown, I would like to add a shower to the tub upstairs. I'll pay for it."

"Oh, I like that!" Connie said.

"Mr. Brown," Elizabeth asked, "as executor of the estate, isn't that within your power?"

"Yes, Bill, you can do that, can't you," Connie interjected.

"Maybe, but as a loving husband, I would want my beautiful wife's approval."

"You may have your shower. I like a shower too sometimes. Now let's finish breakfast and get these papers to Virginia.

"Elizabeth, I have another favor for later today. I would like to borrow the Packard and drive to Athens," Bill said.

"What do you have in mind today?"

"I want to do a little Christmas shopping by myself."

"If I'm on your list, sure."

"Louis Allen is coming to measure for the shower this afternoon. I might be back before he gets here."

"Louis came soon after you left. He said he would be here early tomorrow and should be done by dinner. He said we'd have to buy a rack and shower curtain for the tub. What did you buy me?"

"And me," Connie added.

"I went Christmas shopping, so you have to wait until Christmas, and no peeking. Connie that means you too. But I did buy something we will open before Christmas."

"What? Tell us! Show us!" said Connie excitedly.

"Yes, Bill, what did you get?"

"Decorations and lights for our Christmas tree, enough for a big tree. Where should we put it?"

"Bill, Connie, let's put it in the front room at the window so the people on the road can see it. It will tell them there is a new family here."

"I don't know, Betty May. The front room was where Momma held her sessions," Connie said and closed her eyes. She was quiet for a minute, then she said, "Momma says it is alright."

"Done," Elizabeth added.

Bill said, "I'll get to work on the curtains first thing in the morning."

Thursday was a busy day for all. First, Bill took down the heavy black drapes in the front room windows. With light in the room, they saw how dusty it was.

"I don't think Momma ever dusted anything in here but her session table and chairs. I'm going to see if Clara can come and help me.

"See if Travis can come this afternoon and help me get these chairs in the attic," Bill asked.

The plumber came at nine-thirty and was done by noon. The shower worked fine, but they still needed a curtain. Travis came and he and Bill moved the session chairs to the attic.

"I'm beat," Bill said as he walked into the kitchen. "I want a drink; can I fix you a glass of wine?"

"I'm tired too, Bill. We've had a busy day. I think I want a little of your whiskey," Elizabeth answered. "We will eat after a while."

Bill fixed their drinks and sat at the kitchen table. "The front room looks pretty good," he said. "You and Clara did a good job of cleaning a real mess. Now we need some new furniture."

"I know," Elizabeth answered, "but I'm not sure what I want, or what you want. It ought to be our room. Do I hear the shower?"

"Yes, I guess Connie wants to try it out," Bill answered.

"She'll try out mopping the bathroom floor too," Elizabeth said with a laugh.

"This morning, I'm going to put the session table under the bay window and take down the picture of Jesus. Later we will go and cut a tree, and tonight we can decorate it," Bill said.

"Bill you should have bought some small decorations for the tree. The big ones are fine for the bottom of the tree, but we ought to have some small ones on the top. Connie, don't throw tinsel on the tree. Hang it so it falls down like an icicle."

"Yes, ma'am," they answered in chorus.

Connie looked at Bill, "This is her first Christmas tree too. How come she knows so much about how to decorate one?"

Bill didn't answer.

"Let's try the lights," Elizabeth said.

Bill plugged them in, and they all came on.

"Oh, how pretty!" Connie cried.

"They're all on!" Elizabeth added. "I didn't expect that."

"Well, I am a Georgia Tech engineer," Bill answered, and the lights went out.

"Here's the burned out one," Bill said as he held the offending green bulb. "I've got plenty of spares." With the replacement installed the tree came to life again.

"Are you ready for Christmas?" Diane asked as Elizabeth walked into the sheriff's office Monday morning.

"I don't know, Diane. Momma didn't celebrate Christmas. If it hadn't been for Daddy, I don't think we would have had presents. Santa Claus never came to see us. This is all new to me and Connie. Bill bought decorations and put up a tree. It is nice and Connie loves it."

"Buddy told me he could see the lights from the road."

"Good, the front room sure is different with those heavy curtains gone and the tree." Elizabeth paused. "Diane, I want to ask you a big favor."

"What is it?"

"I want to give Bill and me a honeymoon. I know a place we can go. Could Connie stay with you Thursday and Friday nights? I know it is a lot to ask."

"Elizabeth DuBose...No, Elizabeth DuBose Brown, I would be delighted to have Connie stay with me. I'll work tomorrow and take Friday off. Connie and I will find something interesting to do. Having her stay with me would be a treat."

"Thank you, Diane. You've been such a big help to me, to us. You are my only real friend."

Diane called to Virginia as she walked into Hiram Tilley's office in the courthouse. "Virginia, I'm going to take Friday off this week."

At the sound of Diane's voice, Hiram Tilley stood at his door to listen.

"Are you going to do anything special?" Virginia asked.

"I'm going to keep Connie DuBose while Elizabeth and Bill take a little wedding trip," she answered. "They are leaving Thursday and will come back on Saturday afternoon."

Virginia spoke quietly to Diane, "Is Connie as special as they say? I think Tilley is scared of her."

Diane glanced at Tilley's door and answered Virginia in the same voice, "She knows things about people she has no reason to know. Bill swears she healed his arm—twice. But mostly she is a ten-year-old little girl who had a really strange mother. We'll do some regular things."

"Well, you girls have fun," Virginia said in a normal tone. And quietly added, "You can tell me all about it next week."

Hiram Tilley pushed his door closed and sat at his desk. *Well,*

*well, well, no one is going to be at the DuBose house on Thursday af-
ternoon and all-day Friday. That might be a good time for the County
Clerk to make an evaluation of the property. I'll go tell John at the
bank.* He stood, then sat down. *No, maybe I won't tell John. I'll just
go, but I won't drive to the house. The Graddick place is vacant. I can
drive in there and walk through the woods. Nobody will see my car.*

"Travis is bringing Miss Clara," Connie announced as she came
from the front room. "Bill, thank you for getting a Christmas
tree. We needed something special for Christmas."

"You're welcome. This Christmas was special for all of us. It is
a new beginning, isn't it?"

"I guess so. And, thank you for my radio. I listened some last
night, but the static was bad."

"Santa Claus brought you the radio, but I will fix you an aerial to cut down the static. If you take it to Athens, you won't need
an aerial."

"Santa Claus must really know a lot about radios."

"Santa knows a lot about everything, sort of like you. Slip on
your coat and ask Travis to come in with Clara. Elizabeth has a
job for him and Mr. Moses."

"Did y'all have a happy Christmas, Clara?" Elizabeth asked.

"Yes'm. It was real nice. We went to church Christmas Eve
and the children had a nice program. Travis' momma and me
cooked a big Christmas dinner. We like looking at the house and
seeing the Christmas lights in the window."

"Thank you. We have enjoyed them too. I liked decorating for Christmas."

Turning to Travis, Elizabeth said, "Travis I want to do away with the old privy behind the car shed. Can you and your daddy knock it down and fill the hole?"

"Yes'm. Getting it down won't be no big job at all. It might take two days to haul enough dirt to fill it. We can start this evening. Do you want us to save the boards for you?"

"No, I don't see any need for that."

"Clara, I'm gonna tell daddy," Travis said. "We'll be back after while to start on the outhouse."

"Connie, are you packed for your stay in town? Diane said y'all might go to the picture show."

"That'd be okay. Does Diane have a typewriter?"

Bill answered as they got in the car, "Sure. It's on a little table right beside her desk. Why?"

"I want to see how it works, and why the bell rings. Connie, remember. Diane has work to do, so don't bother her or Sheriff DeWitt," Elizabeth said as they stood in the sheriff's office. "Diane, we will be at the Wilcox Hotel in Aiken."

"La-de-dah," Diane responded, "How did you manage such a place?"

"My roommate last year, her daddy is the doorman there. But I had to buy Bill new shoes."

"New shoes?"

"Never mind, I'll tell you later. We will be back in the afternoon on Saturday."

Diane and Connie waved goodbye as the car drove away.

Hiram Tilley watched from the back door of the courthouse. Inside, he said, "Virginia, I'm going to down to White Plains and look at some properties. I won't be back this afternoon, and I may head straight there in the morning."

"Yes sir, Mr. Tilley," Virginia said. *Now there's a nice after Christmas present for me.*

"Daddy, this outhouse is built pretty good. There are some nice wide boards in it. Let's don't bust it up. We can take it apart and save the boards. It won't take much longer," Travis said to Moses.

"If we get the roof off, I think we can knock the walls down in one piece," Moses answered. "Get the sledge."

16

Tilley drove down the overgrown path to the abandoned Graddick house. He worked his way up the hill toward the big oak tree at the turn in the lane. From there, he could see both the front and side door to the house. Moses wagon was at the end of the car shed. *Damn, why the hell is he here.*

He watched as Moses and Travis loaded lumber on to the wagon. It looked to him as if they were bringing it from the car shed. About four o'clock Moses walked to the wagon empty handed, and Travis went to the side door. In a moment, he and a woman came out and headed to the wagon.

Tilley watched. *The boy went right in, so the door wasn't locked and they didn't do anything to lock it. There's enough light left I can look around inside a little. I wonder what they were doing in the car shed.* He crouched down and moved around the tree as the wagon made the turn at the oak.

Almost joyfully, Tilley trotted to the side door. It was unlocked. *I'll look around and figure out where things are today. Tomorrow I'll come and do a good search.* He found Jefferson's desk in the front bedroom upstairs and decided it would be his starting point. He figured out which bedroom was Connie's and started in, but as soon as he crossed the threshold, he began to feel sweaty. He turned and walked out. *There's enough light left for me to see what those boys were doing in the car shed.*

After a look around, he hadn't found where they had gotten the wood they loaded on the wagon. *Too dark now, I'm going home.*

Around the corner of the shed, Tilley could still make out the shape of the big oak's bare limbs against a nearly black sky. He started toward it. His right foot didn't hit the ground like he expected, and he called out. Quickly he brought his left leg forward. He didn't fall as much as slid feet first into the opening. The hole tapered, and he went down until his hips wedged. His feet didn't hit the bottom. The side of the hole jammed against his right elbow and held his arm against his chest. His left arm pointed at the sky.

"Help! Help!" *That's useless nobody can hear me. I can't see shit even when I look up, and I can hardly fucking move.* He could move his left arm above the elbow, but it didn't touch anything. He kicked with his feet, but they only moved a few inches forward and back before touching the side. Moving his feet caused him to slip down an inch at the hips, but his arms didn't move. The stretch hurt his left shoulder. *Damn my arm hurts. If I move much, I might slide deeper. Hiram be still and think.*

A half-hour later, *this ain't a well, it stinks too bad. I've fallen in a fucking privy. Unless they come here in the morning, I'm going to die in this shit hole. Goddamn, goddamn. Our Father who art in heaven...*

Travis walked into Moses' cabin, "Daddy with this rain, ain't no sense in trying to get dirt for filling the privy today. I've got some little chores I can do in the barn."

"This rain done come in from the east. It may set in. We mightn't get anything done on Saturday."

The cold rain ran down Tilley's up-stretched left arm and onto his chest. It woke him. He fought to remain unconscious, but the pain in his arm and the light wouldn't let him. In the first few seconds, he reconstructed his awful predicament. *Hell, they won't come in this rain. I'm a dead man.* Hiram Tilley wept.

The rain came harder. Tilley's left arm slipped as the water changed the dirt and filth to slick. His hips acted like a cork in a bottle, and he could feel the level moving up his belly toward his chest. *I'm going to fucking drown in shit water. Our Father...* In frustration, he kicked and kicked. The water at his hips had loosened the soil and turned into mud. His kicking released his hips and Tilley slid further down the privy until his feet passed through the two feet of the muck at the bottom of the shaft and rested on mostly solid ground. He screamed in pain as his left shoulder was pushed against his head as he slid down.

The bottom of the shaft was a little wider than the narrow space where his hips had been stuck. Now he could move his right arm and hand. His slide was three feet so his head was now in the narrow neck. Tilley knew he could turn if he could move his left arm. He worked his right hand to his face and scratched away the muddy soil to enlarge the opening. An hour of work let him free his left arm and bring it down by his side. Tilley stood nearly knee deep in the filth at the bottom of the DuBose privy, a cold December rain hit him and water slowly filled the pit. He was cold, soaked to the skin, and his arms ached. *I'm going to die.*

He pressed his back against the side and nearly sat. He waited. *Our Father…*

"Here's Betty May and Bill," Connie called to Diane.

"They are here earlier than I expected," Diane answered. "I guess they've had rain for two days too. Connie, open the door for Elizabeth."

"How was the Wilcox?" Diane asked as Elizabeth stepped in.

"It was as nice as the Drake in New York, but the people were nicer, and I liked the food better. There were a bunch of Yankees down for Christmas," Elizabeth answered.

"Did it rain all day yesterday there?" Diane asked.

"Yes, it was okay. We didn't have any outdoor activities planned."

Connie walked in with her little case, "Did you read? I like to read on a cold, rainy day. That's what we did yesterday afternoon."

Diane added, "We did, and we had a nice day."

"Diane, thank you for having Connie over. You have come through again for us."

Connie added her thank you, and she and Elizabeth walked to the car. The rain had stopped.

As Bill put his suitcase on the bed, Connie came to the door, "I don't know, Betty May. Something's not right in our house."

"What do you mean?" Bill asked.

"It's like somebody was in my room who wasn't supposed to be there."

"Do you think someone came in and took something?" Elizabeth asked.

"No, I looked at my money and my gold cross, and they were there. I don't think they took anything. But somebody was in our house, and it doesn't feel like they've gone either."

"You two stay in this room. I'm going to take a look around."

They heard him opening doors in every room upstairs. "I'm going down stairs now. Stay here," Bill said as he walked by the bedroom door. In a few minutes, he was back. "Connie, there's no one in the house, I promise."

In the kitchen, Connie said, "They're not in the house, but they are still here and, something's wrong. Bill come with me." Connie started for the door.

"Connie, put on a coat. It's cold," Elizabeth called but Connie was gone.

Bill grabbed his hat and coat and followed Connie. He saw her turn behind the car shed.

"Hurry, Bill, hurry!" Connie called.

When he passed the corner of the shed, he saw Connie looking into the privy. "Somebody's down this hole. They're hurt."

"Don't get so close. The ground is wet and slippery. Be careful." Bill stood over the hole and let his eyes adjust to the darkness at the bottom. "I see. It does look like someone." He called, "Hello, can you hear me?"

There was no answer.

Connie said, "I think he moved. I don't think he's dead. We have to get him out."

"Yes, we do." Into the hole, he called, "We see you, and we are going to get help. Hang on."

"Come with me. You need a coat. I'm going to get my flashlight and get Elizabeth to call the sheriff."

When Bill and Connie came from the house, they saw Moses' wagon in the lane coming toward the house. Travis was with him. Bill called and waved to them to hurry.

Before reaching the hole, Bill yelled, "We've got help coming." The light showed a man almost sitting with his head bowed and forward over his knees. His arms were at his sides. The privy was about twelve feet deep. At the ground, the opening was two feet or a little more across.

"Can you hear me?" Bill called, "Can you move? Move anything to give us a signal."

Connie looked down. "Bill, he's the one who was in the house. He is alive, but he's bad sick."

"What's the matter, Deputy Brown?" Travis asked. "We was coming to check on things after all the rain yesterday."

"Somebody fell in."

"Fell in the privy? Daddy come quick. Bring the wagon. Who is it?"

"I don't know."

Elizabeth came from the house, "They're going to find the sheriff and Dr. Parker and send the fire truck."

"We can't wait. The man is dying," Connie cried out.

"He can't be in good shape, that's for sure," Bill said.

"Daddy, if you tie a rope to my legs and let me down, maybe I can get a hold, y'all can pull us out. Or, you can tie to the wagon and let the mules pull us out." Moses tied Travis' legs, and he crawled head first down into the privy.

"Daddy, I can't get past this narrow part, and my arms won't reach him. He's alive. I can hear him breathing. Pull me out now."

"Travis, could you put a rope around him, under his arms?" Bill asked.

"No sir, I don't think I could get down far enough. I'm too big."

"We can dig the hole bigger, but we will have to be careful because dirt will fall on top of him. We'll have to go slow."

"We don't have time," Connie said as she walked to the hole, took off her coat and crawled in head first. She slid down to the narrow part and stopped herself by sticking her legs and arms out.

Elizabeth screamed, "Connie!"

I hear voices calling and see a light. It's my daddy. My daddy is calling me home to heaven. Oh, it's dark again. I need to pray harder. Our Father...Somebody is here. It is an angel to take me home to my daddy and momma in heaven.

"Give me the rope with the loop," Connie called.

The three men looked at one another and then at the little girl calling to them from the privy.

"I said, give me the rope with the loop! I can put it around him. Hurry."

Moses moved first. "Tie this to the wagon axle, Travis." He walked to the edge of the hole. "Miss Cornelia, iffen you can, slip this around his head and get it under his arms. Pull the loop tight on his chest."

"Shine the light down here, Bill." Connie took the rope and

moved deeper into the pit. "Keep moving the light," she called. "I've got him." As she brought her head up, her feet slipped, and she slid toward the bottom. "Ugh," a pause, "I'm all right."

"Miss Cornelia," Moses called, "I'm gonna start pulling. You watch and see he don't get caught. Sing out iffen I need to stop the mules."

A muffled, "Okay," came from the privy.

"Walk 'em easy, Travis. They know this is important."

The rope tightened and Connie called, "He's coming. It's like he's standing."

I'm going up. I'm going up to heaven pulled by an angel. Praise Jesus.

"Travis, whoa."

"Okay, he's up," Connie called.

Bill shined the light onto Tilley, "Moses, the rope's under his arms. You can bring him out."

"Miss Cornelia, hold on to him. Keep his arms down. We're gonna get both of you out at the same time." When she answered, Moses said, "Travis, start the boys pulling, but keep it slow."

As soon as Connie's feet neared the top, Moses called to Travis to stop. Bill reached down and picked Connie up. Elizabeth came running and began wiping the filth from her face with her dress.

The mules pulled another two feet. Moses dropped down and grabbed Tilley under the arms and lifted him, so they were nearly face to face.

Tilley's eyes flickered, "Saint Peter?"

"No boy, I'm Moses. Peter got the day off."

Tilley collapsed in his arms. Moses lifted him and put him in the bed of the wagon.

"I need to touch him, Betty May. His heart was almost gone," Connie said as she broke from her sister and ran to the wagon. In the bed of the wagon, she unbuttoned Tilley's shirt and put her hands on the white bare skin over his heart. "Get some covers for him!"

"Mr. Bill," Moses said, "I know his face is blacker than me right now, but his chest is white. I think it's Mr. Tilley from the court house."

They heard the fire truck well before it appeared. Stevie would run the siren anytime he could. By the time he had gotten to Godfrey's Store Road, he led a small convoy. The truck stopped at the lane so Sheriff DeWitt's car could pass. As he turned, Sheriff DeWitt stopped and told Stevie not to drive to the house unless they called him. He was disappointed but was heartened when the sheriff told him he was in charge of keeping the other cars out.

At the car shed, Bill said, "Ben, we got him out. Dr. Parker, he's in Moses' wagon with Connie. She went in after him."

In the wagon, Dr. Parker looked at Connie who still had her hands under the blanket and on Tilley's chest. "Are you all right?" he asked.

"Yes, sir," she answered, "and he's better. His heart is beating more since I warmed it."

"Ben," Dr. Parker said, "get on the radio and get somebody to call and get Fred out here with the hearse. This man's got to go to the hospital in Athens."

Before Ben answered, Elizabeth said, "I will call the funeral home from the house."

Dr. Parker looked over at Travis whose clothes were covered with the nasty blackness of the privy. "Did you go down in the hole?" he asked.

"Yes, sir, but only one time."

Dr. Parker instructed, "Moses, as soon as we get this man out of your wagon, take your boy home. Travis, when you get home wash. Scrub every inch of yourself good with soap and hot water. If you don't burn these clothes, boil them. Don't let anyone else touch them either. And don't touch your baby until you've bathed."

"I got Pete," Elizabeth said when she came from the house, "He's on his way. He knows you want to go to Athens."

For the first time, Sheriff DeWitt took charge. "Let's get this man out of Moses' wagon so he can take Travis home. Anybody got any idea who he is?"

Bill answered, "Moses says he looks like Hiram Tilley."

"Tilley?" Sheriff DeWitt asked. "I thought it was a colored man. But Tilley's wife said he didn't come home Thursday night. What would Tilley be doing out here?"

Connie answered from the wagon where she continued to keep her hands on the man's chest, "Mr. Tilley wanted our house. I didn't like him, but I don't want him to die."

At the wagon, Ben said, "For sure that's a white man's hair, and it does look like Tilley." *I need a long talk with John Harwell.*

The four men lifted Tilley from the wagon and laid him on blankets on the ground and covered him with more.

Dr. Parker said, "You saved this man's life. You and Travis and

Moses. Now you go and wash like I told Travis. I'll take care of
Mr. Tilley."

In another twenty minutes, they had Tilley in Fred Thompson's hearse. "Pete, I'll ride in the back here with Tilley. You don't
have to race, but don't tarry." Then out the window, "Ben, be sure
and call the hospital. Talk to Dr. Allen if you can. Let's go."

Ben looked at Bill, "You and Elizabeth come see me on
Monday. That'll be soon enough. Now, I've got to tell Martha
Tilley about all of this."

17

All slept late on Sunday, Connie until nearly ten o'clock. "Where's Bill?" she asked when she came down.

"He has the clothes you had on yesterday. He is going to drop them in the old privy, pour oil on them and burn them there. How do you feel this morning?"

"I feel good, and Mr. Tilley isn't going to bother us anymore about our house, but he's not going to die."

"Good," Elizabeth answered as Bill came in. "Connie says Mr. Tilley isn't going to bother us anymore."

"His mind is all different now. He thinks he died and went to Heaven, met Moses, and came back alive. He wants to tell everybody Moses is a colored man, and he was pulled to heaven by an angel with a rope."

"If he spent two nights and a day alone at the bottom of a privy, he may have lost his mind. I've seen it happen to pilots when it has taken time to find them after a crash," Bill said.

"Betty May, I know we have a good house, but why would he want it so bad?" Connie asked.

"Connie, and you too, Bill. I've always heard talk in town

Momma or Daddy hid a treasure here, a railroad car load of money," Elizabeth answered.

"I've heard it too," Bill said.

"Bill, I don't know anything about that. Daddy never told me anything and he told me a lot about running the house. Momma never said anything either. I found some papers where Daddy kept records on the railroad cars. They show everybody got what they deserved."

"Betty May, I never thought about a secret treasure," Connie said.

"There's somebody driving here," Connie called from the front room where she was taking decorations off the tree. "I think it's Mr. Hall."

"Ask him in. I'll be right there."

"Who's coming?" Bill asked as he came in from the car shed.

"Connie says it's Orren Hall," Elizabeth answered.

"I think the last time I talked with him was when I was the deputy. He and my daddy were friends."

Connie opened the door before Orren Hall could knock. "Come in, Mr. Hall. Betty May and Bill are coming."

"Thanks, Connie. You know my boy Paul, don't you?"

"Yes, sir," Connie answered as she looked at Paul. *He looks different today, he's tall and his hair is kinda gold, not white.*

Paul smiled and managed, "Hey, Connie. Are you going to stay awake to see the new year come in?"

"Hello, Paul." *He was in third grade when I first went to school, so he's twelve now. He's pretty.* "I don't think so. I get sleepy."

"Me neither. Daddy wakes me early to help with milking."

As Bill and Elizabeth walk up, Orren said, "Miss Elizabeth, I've come to talk a little business, if I might."

"Certainly," Elizabeth answered. "Let's go in the parlor. Connie why don't you take Paul in the front room. Maybe he can help taking some of the decorations off the tree. As tall as he is, he can reach near the top."

Connie took Paul's hand and led him into the front room. *Betty May knows he's tall too.*

"Which ones should I get?"

"Any near the top."

"I need both hands to reach high."

Connie made a disappointed sound and released Paul's hand.

"Should I put them in the box?"

"No, give them to me. I'll put them in."

After a few decorations were moved from the tree to their boxes, Paul ventured, "Did you really jump into the old privy to help Mr. Tilley?"

"I didn't jump. I sorta crawled in."

"Wasn't it nasty and didn't you get really dirty?"

"I didn't think about any of that. The man was about to die." Connie thought about the dirty part and added, "but I've had three baths since, good hot baths. I'm really clean now. You don't have to worry about me being dirty."

"I'm not worried about you being dirty. You were brave. Daddy says you saved his life."

"He was going to die soon if he didn't get out. Now he is alive, but I don't think he is the same. He used to be mean and want our house, and now he doesn't care."

Paul handed Connie several more balls from the tree. "That's all I can reach. Deputy Brown will have to get the rest."

Connie took Paul's hand again, "They're still talking. We can sit here." She led him to the two side by side chairs. "Are you in the seventh grade now?"

"Yeah."

"I'm going to be in the fifth grade in Athens when school starts next week. Betty May is going to college."

"Are y'all moving?"

"We'll stay in Athens for school but come home on Friday afternoon. We have an apartment."

Mr. Hall looked in, "Paul, let's go. Bill, Elizabeth, thank you."

"Yes, sir," Paul answered his father. "Bye, Connie. I hope you like your school."

"Orren, this will be good for Elizabeth, you, and for her property," Bill said as Orren and Paul walked out the door.

"What will be good?" Connie asked.

"Mr. Hall wants to buy some more cows to milk and needs more pasture. He is going to rent our land by the creek. He'll pay rent and take care of the fences," Elizabeth answered.

"It would be real good if Paul could bring the rent money."

18

Bill Brown transitioned to the Air Force when it was formed in September 1947. He remained at MIT until he completed his Master's in May 1948. Assigned to the Pentagon, he worked on air war plans for a likely conflict with North Korea. In May of 1949, he was promoted to Lieutenant Colonel. Bill's rank, job, and connections allowed him to get home to Greensboro often.

Elizabeth and Connie split their time between Athens and school and their home in Greensboro. With summer sessions, Elizabeth finished her bachelor's degree in May 1948. Since Bill's immediate future was uncertain, she began a master's program in Economics.

Connie adapted well to public school and finished the seventh grade.

With no summer session in August, Elizabeth and Connie returned to Greensboro for the end of the summer. Bill joined them there for the last two weeks.

Most afternoons, Connie watched to see when Paul came to get the cows for milking. She ran to the creek, met him, and walked on her side. They could talk in a normal voice because the creek wasn't big. Connie liked it because on her side the bank was three or four feet higher than Paul's bottom land side. They walked as far as the hill where the creek turned toward Paul's side and flowed through the bottom.

At the turn, the bank on Connie's side rose a few more feet above the water with big trees right to the edge. On the other side, the creek widened. A spit of gravel and sand made a tiny beach in the bend.

Three o'clock on a hot afternoon, Connie saw Paul at the gate. *Boy, it is early for him to get the cows. I wonder if something is wrong.* Connie knew she would never catch up with him, so she headed straight for the place where the creek turned. She beat him to the spot and could see him coming through the pasture. She stepped into the shadow of a big sycamore tree.

Paul's blond hair disappeared as the path dipped and reappeared like a white rising sun pushed up by his slender body. In full view now and standing at the edge of the gravel, he was not more than thirty feet from her. Connie started to call but stopped as his hand went to his fly. Connie dropped her eyes as he unbuttoned. Paul turned away. Peeking, she saw him in a pose she would see often when men and boys were outside. *It is easy for boys outside.* Paul's right arm shook, and he turned back.

A few steps on to the gravel, he stopped and pulled his boots and socks off. He took another step and worked his feet back and forth in the rough sand.

I can't say anything now or he'll know I saw him peeing. I should go.

Paul unhooked one strap from the bib of his overalls and slid the other strap over his arm and stepped out of them, turned and dropped them on his boots. As he turned to the water, he unbuttoned his shirt, slipped out of it and tossed it to the pile.

Connie didn't move. She couldn't move. She didn't think, and even with her gifts, she had no idea what was next. Paul Hall was standing in front of her in nothing but his underwear as close as if he were in the front hall of her house, and she were at the top of the stairs.

Paul turned to the pile and picked up his overalls and pulled out a white lump about the size of an egg. He pushed his underwear down to his thighs. They fell to the ground and he stepped out and added them to the other clothes. His butt and legs were dead white. His shoulders were a little tan and the outline of his overalls showed from the times he had worked in the sunshine with no shirt. Below the length of shirt sleeves his arms were dark.

I like his white butt. No, I'm not supposed to think that. He is going to turn around. I'll close my eyes. Paul turned toward the water. Connie closed her eyes…for an instant. *His front is as white as his butt. And his hair is blond like on his head. Elizabeth's is red like her head, makes sense.*

Paul stepped into the water. He was only knee deep, and he was much closer to Connie. *If I move, he will see me.* He moved his feet around like he was looking for something on the bottom. When he didn't find anything, he turned down stream and sat. For a few minutes he let the cool water flow around his shoulders and take his summer heat into the bottom.

Connie breathed out, maybe for the first time in minutes. She was relieved she wasn't looking at his naked body, but she was disappointed too. How long is he going to sit there like that? The wait wasn't long. He brought one hand out and rubbed his other arm with it. He had the white lump in his hand. *It is soap. He's taking a bath.*

He stood and washed one leg and then the other and turned slightly toward Connie. He started between his legs and worked up a little lather. He rubbed the soap on his chest and arms changing hands to get everything.

If he had a washcloth it would be easier. I like the way he looks wet.

Sitting down, he leaned forward and ducked his head under, and rubbed his head with his fingers. When he came up his blond hair looked dark and was all tangled. He rubbed the soap bar on his head.

I would wash his hair with real shampoo.

He ducked under again and when he came up, his hair was still dark, but a bit less tangled.

You're supposed to wash it twice, Paul.

He stood and moved a step closer to Connie's bank. He reached between his legs and looked at what he was holding. Connie did too.

It's little, littler than when he got in the water. I shouldn't be watching. I have to go. I can't. He'll see me and tell. I won't look. But she did. *He's going to pee where he took a bath. I know I don't want to watch him pee.*

Paul didn't pee. He lathered again.

He washed it once. Do they get that dirty? Elizabeth says I should wash good, but twice in one bath. He should have washed his hair twice. Even with the lather there, Connie realized Paul was not washing. He was holding and rubbing. What had been small was now big, real big. *I've seen boy babies and Daddy and Bill once, but I've never seen anything like this. Is it hurt?* Connie looked to Paul's face. His eyes were closed and he had a strange expression on his face. *That's not hurt, he likes it.*

She noticed his left hand was on his chest over his nipple. Her eyes went to his busier right hand. *What's he doing? I usually know about things… but, but.* Connie realized her right hand was between her legs and her legs were holding it tightly, and her left was rubbing her nipple. *What am I doing?* She moved her left hand and looked at Paul.

Her left hand returned to her chest, and she shifted her weight slightly from leg to leg against her right hand. Paul's hand seemed to be moving faster now, and he dropped his head. *He's looking at it if his eyes are open.* As close as they were Connie couldn't tell about his eyes. But she watched what she thought he was watching. Paul said something.

My God, he has seen me. Connie froze. *I'm not supposed to swear.*

Paul said something else, and Connie looked at him. She realized it wasn't a word, only a sound. And there was another. Now his head was facing the sky, and she could see his eyes were closed. She chanced shifting her legs again. His right hand was moving fast now, another sound.

Paul opened his eyes and looked down at his hand and smiled. He sat in the water for a few seconds and ducked his head. When he came out, he walked to his clothes on the bank. He ran his fingers through his hair and let the sun dry it and him.

It's regular size now. And she squeezed her hand hard with her legs. Paul dressed quickly and headed into the bottom. When he disappeared, Connie relaxed and stepped away from the sycamore tree. She looked at her hands and to where she had last seen Paul. *I don't know, Betty May, I don't know. I usually know.*

I have to go pray. I know looking at Paul naked was a sin. I don't know which one, but it has to be a sin. I shouldn't like sin, but I liked looking at his butt. And I took the Lord's name in vain. I didn't say it out loud, but I said it.

At the house, she went to the front room and knelt under the painting of Saint Paul. Connie asked for forgiveness for taking the Lord's name in vain, for not knowing what her sin was and strength to not want to see Paul naked again.

Bill and Elizabeth had driven to Athens to shop, mostly to restock the bar. They got home about five o'clock. It was too hot for much cooking and there were fresh tomatoes from Moses' garden. Elizabeth fried bacon for sandwiches. As they were finishing, Connie looked at Bill, "I want to ask you something about boys."

Bill knew two things about Connie's questions, they were never simple and they had to be answered. "Sure." he said.

Connie continued, "Today I saw Paul going to get the cows early, and I walked to the creek to see him like I do some time."

"Okay."

"Well, I got to the place where the creek turns and waited for him. But when he got there, I didn't say anything, and he didn't see me. Anyway, he took off all his clothes and took a bath with soap."

Elizabeth looked at her sister, "It wasn't very nice to watch him. Being naked is a private thing."

"I know, Betty May, and I came home and prayed about what I did and asked the Lord to forgive me. And I asked Him to help me not do it again, because I liked it."

With as much indignity as she could muster, Elizabeth questioned, "You liked seeing him naked?"

"Yes, I did, Betty May. I know it is a sin and that's why I prayed so hard."

"And you better keep praying," she said, biting her lip.

Bill's joy at watching his young wife's discomfort ended when Connie looked at him and said, "Bill seeing Paul naked wasn't what I wanted to ask about. When he finished and he had washed everywhere. He stood and put some more soap on his, his... you know."

"Penis?"

"Yes, penis. And he washed it. But really, I don't think he was washing as much as rubbing it. And it got big, really big."

No longer on the verge of laughter now, Elizabeth asked, "And you watched?"

"I did. At first, I thought he might be hurt. But when I looked at his face, I could tell he wasn't. In a few minutes he made a sound, and he smiled and sat in the water. When he stood his, his penis was regular. Bill, is Paul alright?"

"Yes, he is fine."

"Well, what was he doing?"

"He was masturbating." Bill was going to continue, but Connie interrupted.

"Does it have something to do with fishing? It didn't look like fishing."

"No, it doesn't have anything to do with fishing." And Bill paused.

"Bill?" Connie asked.

"Yes, Bill?" Elizabeth added, clearly now enjoying his discomfort.

"It is a way someone can give themselves pleasure. If feels good."

"It must feel real good from the way he looked," Connie said. "Did he have to do it in the water?"

"No," Bill answered, "but it is something people do in private."

"People? Can girls do masturbating? Is that the way to say it?" And Connie looked at Elizabeth.

"Yes."

"Girls?" questioned Connie.

"Yes, girls too. I see we have some more growing up things to talk about," Elizabeth said.

Connie was quiet for a few minutes and Bill and Elizabeth relaxed. But it was too soon. In a burst of awareness, Connie asked, "Betty May, does this masturbating thing have anything to do with what you told me about babies and getting your period and all of that? Are you supposed to wait until you are married to masturbate?"

Elizabeth answered, "Yes, it has something to do with all of that."

And Bill added, "Connie you don't have to wait until you are married, and it is not a sin. But it is a private thing. I don't think Paul would like it if he knew you watched him."

"I'll apologize to him."

Both Bill and Elizabeth answered "No." together, and Elizabeth added. "Don't say anything, but don't do it again."

"I won't, but I did…It was exciting and I had some good feelings.

19

In May 1950, Bill was ordered to Okinawa, Japan. He was to leave June 6.

Elizabeth received her Master's in Economics in May, and she and Connie planned to spend the summer in Greensboro. Since Bill was going to be overseas, Elizabeth accepted a graduate assistant's position at the University of South Carolina where she could work on her doctorate.

Elizabeth needed one more trip to Athens to get the last of their things from the apartment.

"Are you sure you don't mind staying here by yourself all afternoon?" Elizabeth asked as she and Bill walked to the Packard.

"I'll be fine. I like the quiet, and I might read some." answered Connie. "Y'all go on. Maybe you can bring me something, a surprise."

"If you left anything in the apartment, that'll be your surprise," Bill said.

"Bye, bye, Bill." Connie said. She added a dismissive wave.

"Your little sister is beginning to act like my wife."

"I've tried to be a good example."

In the front hall, Connie walked to the double doors of the front room where her mother used to hold her sessions. Then there were heavy drapes at the windows and the double pocket doors always stayed closed. Now the room was bright and airy with new furniture. Elizabeth and Connie kept the *Conversion of St. Paul* altarpiece as a reminder of their mother's reverence for the Apostle. They didn't move it but added a small table underneath with candles and their mother's Bible.

Connie resisted the urge to go into the front room. Instead, she went to her bedroom and came down with her new Nancy Drew, *The Clue of the Leaning Chimney*. She liked to read in her Momma's big chair in the corner of the parlor, but today she couldn't get into her book. She knew her mother was calling her, and she had to go into the front room.

Standing in front of the altarpiece she held her mother's Bible and closed her eyes. Immediately she had a vision of Travis Jackson's cabin. His wagon was there, and she could see Travis, Clara, their four-year-old daughter, Moses, Liza, and several others. They all had their heads bowed. In the back of the wagon was a small wooden box she knew was a coffin for Travis and Clara's new baby boy. As the images faded, Connie realized she was seeing a scene in the fading light of dusk.

This hasn't happened yet. I still have time. She heard her mother's voice, "Go."

Connie ran out the front door and down the nearly quarter mile drive. When she reached the road, she met Liza's sister, Corina, and her husband in their wagon. Angel and Harrison, two of their grands, were in the back.

"Miss Cornelia, is something the matter? You look plum out of breath," asked Corina.

"My Momma told me I had to go to Travis' house. There's something wrong with his new baby. Momma wants me to help."

It was of no concern to Corina that Connie's mother had been dead for nearly four years. "Get in child, we are going there now. The baby's got the fever that's going around. Dr. Parker says all we can do is pray."

Angel helped Connie climb in and sit on the flat bed of the wagon. She said, "If your Momma say to help, I know you can do something. I don't want Travis' baby boy to die."

Harrison looked at his older sister. "You say her Momma be dead a long time, how she gonna tell her to help?"

"Harrison, you hush up," corrected Corina. "Miss Cornelia's got gifts. The Holy Spirit lets her talk to her Momma."

Angel added, "And she can help sick people get well."

"We need to pray for the baby. Angel, what is his name?"

"Aaron, like in the Bible."

"I'm going to pray right now."

Corina's husband Tom pulled on the reins to stop the wagon.

"Oh, don't stop," said Connie, "Keep going, we need to get there quick. God won't mind if you watch the road while I pray."

Tom popped the reins lightly and the wagon lurched forward with a little more speed. Connie rolled to her knees, folded her hands and bowed her head. Angel took the same position beside her. Ten-year-old Harrison remained sprawled out with his back to the side of the wagon. Corina bowed her head.

Connie started "Our Father, our brother Aaron is suffering." A few more sentences about how his family loved God followed, then Connie spoke in words and phrases only she and the Lord understood. Corina added a "Praise Jesus," and Angel a "Hallelujah." Hearing Connie's prayer, Harrison thought better of his profane posture, scrambled to his knees beside Connie, folded his hands and bowed his head. The wagon turned toward the Jackson's cabins. Connie prayed until they reached Mt. Nebo Church.

Corina turned in her seat and looked at Connie. Connie was pale and her hair was sticking to her forehead and the sides of her face. "Come here, Miss Cornelia, and let me clean you up." Connie knee walked to her, and Corina wiped her face gently with a handkerchief.

Connie looked at Corina and said, "Aaron is bad sick. The fever will burn up his brain. Hurry, Mr. Tom. Aaron needs me."

Tom popped the reins and got the mule to a trot. Before he could stop the wagon, Connie jumped out and ran into the cabin without acknowledging Moses, Travis, or any of the men in the yard.

The cabin was dark. All the curtains were pulled and there was no lantern or candle lit. Connie's eyes went immediately to the bed on the side of the room. She could make out baby Aaron lying on his back hardly moving. From across the room she could hear the soft rattle of his labored breaths. Liza wiped his face with a damp cloth. Clara sat in a rocking chair beside the bed with her face in her hands. There were two other ladies there.

All had looked to the light when Connie opened the door. They stared at the shape of a small white girl with stringy hair.

Clara stood as Connie closed the door behind her. "Momma sent me to help." And she walked to the bed where Aaron lay.

"Miss Clara, may I sit in the rocker?" Connie asked.

"Yes'm."

Connie unbuttoned her shirt and took it off and slipped off a camisole. She put her shirt on but didn't button it and sat in the rocker. "Please, give Aaron to me."

Without hesitation, Liza took her grandson. He whimpered at being disturbed and the rattle of his breath was louder. She placed Aaron in Connie's outstretched arms. Connie kissed him on the forehead, and the whimpering eased. She pulled him against her bare chest and started the chair rocking. Looking first at Liza and then at Aaron's mother, Clara, she said, "We will be here for a while. You look tired. Go and rest." Connie closed her eyes.

The women watched without speaking. In about twenty minutes, Clara sat on the bed. In a few more she went to sleep. Lisa and the two others walked outside to tell the men what was happening. Liza returned and sat in a chair watching Connie and Aaron. She thought Aaron's breathing had quieted some.

"Connie," Elizabeth called as she and Bill came in. When there was no answer, she said, "She might be upstairs."

Bill was carrying a box of odds and ends from the Athens apartment. "Most of these things are hers," he said. "I'll take them to her." When he came down, he said, "Connie is not upstairs. Maybe she went down to the creek to see Paul."

"I don't think so. They were already milking when we came

by. Paul should be at the barn. She may have gone for a walk like she does, but would you ride over and see if she is there."

At the end of the drive, Bill could see where a wagon had stopped and there were foot prints coming from the drive. At Tom and Corina's place, Bill could tell a wagon had come on to the road.

"Hello, Bill. You need some milk?" Orren Hall called as Bill walked into the milking barn.

"No, Orren. I was looking for Connie. I thought she might have come over to see Paul."

"No, we haven't seen her at all. Paul just now went to the house."

Bill turned to the young man who was washing the manure out of the barn. "Tommy, it looked like your daddy's wagon might have stopped at our place this afternoon. Do you know if he was going anywhere?"

Tommy folded the hose over to stop the flow of water. "Yes sir, Deputy Brown. Him and momma and my children gone down to Travis' house. Travis' new baby is real sick with the fever. They don't think he will live through the night. I'm going there as soon as I finish here."

Orren said, "Why didn't you tell me, Tommy? You go on, I'll finish the barn. Go on."

"Yes sir, Mr. Hall, and thank you."

"Get those boots off and I will ride you as far as your place."

"Thank you, Deputy Brown."

On the way to the house Bill realized if Connie knew about Travis' baby, she would have to go. He told Elizabeth what he had learned, and she agreed Connie would go.

Bill didn't drive close to the cabins. He and Elizabeth got out and walked toward them. Moses came out to meet them. Before Bill or Elizabeth could ask about Connie, Moses started talking.

"Miss Cornelia came and said her Momma sent her to help. Liza say she been sitting and rocking the baby since two o'clock." It was now after six.

Two men who stood outside of Travis' cabin nodded respectfully at the daughter of Mary Greene DuBose and the former Greene County deputy as they stepped onto the porch.

Liza greeted Elizabeth and Bill at the door, but she was looking at Bill. Bill waited on the porch with Moses.

"Miss Elizabeth, Miss Cornelia's been sitting with the baby all afternoon. She don't say nothing since she sat down. But the baby don't fret like he did, but he don't move much."

Connie opened her eyes, turned to Elizabeth and smiled.

Elizabeth started toward her, and Connie held up her hand.

"She won't let nobody touch her or the baby."

Still looking at Elizabeth, Connie whispered, "In the morning." She kissed Aaron's head and closed her eyes.

"You go on home, Miss Elizabeth. We won't let anything happen to Miss Cornelia. My cousin's boy has his horse and he can get to you quick."

"Liza, I think we will stay here. We can sleep in the car."

"Yes'm. We will have some supper ready soon and bring you a plate."

During the next hour, the mules were unhitched, fed, watered, and put in Moses' pen. Food was brought from Moses' house, and folks ate in the back of the wagons or on the porches. Elizabeth and Bill got cornbread, a small piece of ham, and sliced tomatoes.

It was getting dark and after eating, the men began to fix places to sleep in and under their wagons.

Bill walked toward the cabins with their empty supper plates. Travis met him and took the plates. At their car, Elizabeth propped in the front seat. Bill stretched out in the big back seat.

The reflection of the headlights of an older Chevrolet on the Packard's window made Bill sit. Travis and one of the others came to the car. Travis called to the cabin, "It's Pastor Manigault."

When the driver stepped out Bill recognized him.

A young man wearing a white shirt and a tie got out on the passenger side. He reached in the car for his suit coat and put it on. Bill watched while Jacob introduced the new man to the group. On the porch, they talked with Travis and his father. The pastor and the new man went in. Bill walked a little closer.

Travis came down to him and told him the other man was a preacher from Atlanta, but was going to school in Pennsylvania, and had come to visit Pastor Manigault.

One oil lamp gave a pale-yellow glow to the room. Connie's head was down with her cheek resting on Aaron's head. Her hands cradled his back.

Jacob spoke. "Miss Cornelia?" And Connie raised her head and opened her eyes. She gave a small smile of recognition, and the pastor stepped toward her. She quickly raised her hand, and he stopped. "We come to pray for the baby and lay on hands."

Connie shook her head "no" and held her finger to her lips.

Liza touched her pastor's elbow and led him toward a corner of the room. As they walked away, she said "Preacher Manigault. she wouldn't even let her sister come close. Aaron's breath is quieter since she's had him. They been sitting all afternoon."

Connie looked at the newcomer and smiled. She could see the ends of his mustache turn up as he smiled at her. She touched her finger to her lips again but held out her hand to him. The young man looked to Preacher Manigault, but he was turned away still talking with Liza. Connie beckoned and extended her hand. Before he took it, she bowed her head and looked to the floor beside her chair. He knelt there as he took her hand.

At first her hand felt cold, dead cold. With his head bowed, he started to pray so quietly no one in the room but Connie could hear. As he talked to the Lord, Connie's hand began to warm, and he felt the warmth move through his arm and into his body.

Connie spoke a word everyone in the room could hear, but no one understood. They all looked to Connie, Aaron, and the young preacher as the preacher added, "Amen, Hallelujah."

Connie's hand now felt hot to the newcomer, and heat flowed into him. He began to sweat. His shirt stuck to his back under his coat, he could feel water pooling against his belt. Perspiration from his bowed head fell in big drops, making spots on the rough floor.

Connie released his hand. Both raised their heads and looked at one another and smiled. The young man slowly stood from his kneeling position but had to pause and get his balance. Standing, he looked down at Connie as she raised her face to him. He bent down and kissed her gently on the lips and turned. "Jacob, help me," he said.

"Martin," Jacob said as he steadied his friend, "you are soaking wet. Let's get to the porch where it is cooler. I'm taking you to my house." Five minutes later they left.

When the sky began to lighten, Clara raised her head. She had slept all night. Connie and Aaron were still there in the chair, but Aaron was moving his arms and turning his head. Connie looked at Clara as Aaron nuzzled her chest. "Momma, I think your boy is hungry. Come, take him."

Clara took her baby. "He's not hot!" she said as she opened her dress. "Oh, and he is hungry. Thank you, Jesus."

Liza walked to the porch and called, "Travis, your baby's better. Miss Cornelia and the Lord done take the fever out of him."

Travis jumped from his wagon where he had spent a restless night and ran to his mother. Moses had slept on the porch. He sat up when his wife walked out, and now he pulled himself up by the corner post. The other men in the dooryard of the cabin roused and looked to Liza.

"Moses," she said, "say a prayer."

Moses, now standing, bowed his head and began praying.

Travis had taken a step toward his mother on the porch but stopped when his daddy started his prayer.

The noise and activity at the porch woke Bill. When all there bowed their heads, he knew the baby had not made it through the night. He opened the car door to listen.

Elizabeth, waking from her fitful sleep, asked, "What's happening?"

"I don't know," Bill replied. "But I don't think it is good. Moses is praying."

By now, both were out of the car and could hear what Moses

said. They realized Moses was giving thanks for the life of the baby. Bill took Elizabeth's hand, and they stood by the car until Moses finished.

Elizabeth ran to the cabin. When Liza saw her, she waved for her to come in. She hurried into the still dark room.

Connie was in the rocker. Her open shirt stuck to her skin and her hair was a mess of damp strings. She was as wet as if someone had poured a bucket of water on her. Connie looked at baby Aaron feeding at Clara's breast and smiled.

Tears streamed down Clara's face, but she wasn't crying.

When Elizabeth got to the chair, Connie looked, smiled, and held out her hand to her. "Betty May," she said, "I'm empty, all poured out."

Elizabeth leaned in and kissed her little sister on the forehead. "Let's go home now," she said.

Elizabeth and Liza helped Connie stand. Elizabeth peeled off the wet shirt and Liza brought a clean cloth and dried Connie's shoulders and back. Elizabeth slipped the camisole on Connie and wrapped the cloth over her shoulders. With Connie between them, Elizabeth and Clara moved to the porch.

"Bill, help us," Elizabeth said. "We need to take Connie home.

Bill looked at Connie. She was pale and trembling. He stepped to her, put one arm around her back and the other under her knees, and lifted her, and he started for the Packard. Bill slipped Connie into the back seat and closed the door. "Let's go," he said.

Driving out Mt. Nebo road, Bill said to Elizabeth, "She is hot. She is hot all over. It feels more than fever hot."

Connie slept all day. At supper time Elizabeth and Bill heard the toilet flush, and Elizabeth went upstairs.

"I'm still sleepy, Betty May, and I'm not hungry," Connie said as she climbed into her bed. "I'm okay."

"I looked in her room this morning," Elizabeth said. "Her color seemed better and her breathing was quiet. I slipped in and touched her forehead and she didn't feel hot."

"That's good," Bill answered. "If she doesn't get up soon, maybe you can take her a little food."

They heard the toilet and a few minutes later, the shower.

"That's a good sign," Bill said.

"Yes, but I'm going to check," Elizabeth answered. When she returned, she said, "Connie says she's hungry and wants scrambled eggs."

"She ought to be hungry. It's been nearly two days since she's eaten anything."

"Bill, it has been a good twenty minutes since the shower stopped. I'm going to see if she went back to bed."

As Elizabeth stood, they heard Connie's footsteps on the stairs. When she came into the kitchen she was dressed, and her hair was brushed.

"Is there any coffee left. I think I want a cup of coffee," Connie said as she entered the kitchen.

"Yes," Bill answered. "I'll fix it for you, sit down. Besides hungry, how do you feel?"

"Hungry."

Connie sat sipping her coffee as Elizabeth finished the eggs and served the plate. She ate about half the eggs and ham on her plate. "I think I want some milk."

As she started to stand, Bill said, "Sit, I'll get your milk. Anything else?"

"Do we have any blackberry jam?"

"Yes," Elizabeth answered, "I'll get it."

As she pushed away the now empty plate, Connie said, "That was good. I do feel much better now. But Bill and Betty May, something is different. I feel good, but something is different about me."

"What do you mean?" Elizabeth asked.

"Baby Aaron—I should know how he is, but I don't. I don't know or feel anything about him now. And last night, I came downstairs to talk to mother, and I couldn't."

"Don't you think it's because you are tired?" Elizabeth asked.

"It feels different than tired. I don't know."

"I think I hear a wagon," Bill said. He walked to the door. "It is Moses."

Connie ran to the door and out ahead of Bill. "Mr. Moses. Mr. Moses, please tell me about Aaron. Is he alright?"

As Moses climbed down from the wagon, he said, "Baby Aaron be fine, Miss Cornelia. That's what I come to tell you." Looking, he called to Bill, "Mr. Bill, I come to speak to Miss Cornelia, if it be suitable."

"Sure," Bill called and went into the kitchen.

"Aaron is doing good, Miss Cornelia. Clara say he is eating good and he breathes quiet and easy, but he sleeps more than usual. How are you?"

"I'm good. I slept until this morning and Betty May fixed me a big breakfast, but I think I'm going to take a nap later."

"Miss Cornelia, we know it was the Lord who helped Aaron, but we know the Holy Spirit had to come on you for the Lord to help."

"Mr. Moses, that's what Momma always told me I had to do. It is my responsibility, my gift."

"I know, Miss Cornelia. We do. But me and Travis are going to look out for you from now on. You helped to save my grand's life, and he carries my name, Moses Aaron Jackson. As much as we can, you will be in our keeping."

Connie looked at Moses and saw tears running down his cheeks. She stepped closer and put her arms around him, "Thank you, Mr. Moses, thank you. I love you and the Lord loves you."

Moses moved his arms from his side and to Connie's back and pulled her a little closer, "Thank you, Miss Cornelia. Now, I gots to go." He stepped away and climbed on his wagon and turned it without looking to Connie.

As she walked into the kitchen Connie announced, "Mr. Moses says baby Aaron is doing good. I'm going to take a nap."

20

Bill is still in Japan coordinating bombing missions into North Korea. He seldom flies, but Elizabeth worries. She and Connie have an apartment in Columbia near the University of South Carolina. Connie has finished the ninth grade at University High School. When the school-year ends, they return to Greensboro for the month of June.

The seven miles from Union Point to Greensboro seemed the longest part of the trip from Columbia. "Hurry, Betty May," Connie said, "I need to go to the bathroom."

"We'll stop at the sheriff's office to see Diane. She'll let you use theirs. I won't be long. You can walk to Hunter's and get a Coke if you want," Elizabeth answered.

"Betty May, I almost feel like a stranger in Greensboro now. I don't know anybody, no kids anyway. Maybe I will see somebody at Hunter's."

Connie ran to the door of the sheriff's office, and when she saw only Diane in the office, she called, "Where's the bathroom? I need to go bad."

"Ma'am," Diane said as she stood and turned to the door, "We don't have a public bath...Damn, Cornelia DuBose, look at you. You are not a little girl anymore. That's a cute skirt, and you have on lipstick. I guess you grow up quick in a big city like Columbia." Diane pointed, "Down the hall."

The door opened again, and Elizabeth walked in. Connie disappeared.

"It is a long drive from Columbia," Elizabeth said. "We are both tired, but I want to talk with you."

"Elizabeth, you sure don't have a little sister anymore."

"No, I guess not. It all started last summer soon after she spent the night with the Jackson baby. That night changed her."

"What do you mean?" asked Diane.

"Besides growing up, she doesn't seem to get the strong feelings about people or know things like she used to. This year was tough enough without her 'gift'. I don't know if I could have made it if she knew what I was thinking."

"No mother I know says that time is fun, or their little darlings are cute. And, you are only a sister," Diane added.

"At least all the changes were quick. She is not too comfortable with everything yet. She doesn't know what to do about the attention she gets from boys."

"I can understand the attention. She really is pretty, and dressed in a skirt and blouse, she looks much older than fourteen."

"I am going to walk to Hunter's," Connie said as she came from the hall.

Elizabeth answered, "I'm not going to be long. I will find you."

"Did you see anybody?" Elizabeth asked.

"No, there weren't any kids there, besides the last time I went to school with any Greensboro kids was when I was in the third grade, six years ago."

"We need milk," Elizabeth said as she turned into the Hall's dairy. "Here's a quarter. We will have to bring our jug back."

Connie pushed the door to the milk house open, and Paul Hall was filling gallon Coca Cola jugs with fresh milk. "Paul."

Paul turned in the dim light of the milk room to see the silhouette of a woman in the door. "Who is it?" he asked.

"Paul, it's me, Connie. Connie DuBose."

As Connie walked into the milk room and out of the glare, Paul's eyes adjusted. Even in the light, Paul had a hard time resolving the figure before him and his memories of the little girl from the house on the hill. His confusion and hormones did nothing to make him comfortable. "Yes, I see. Connie, it is you." After a pause that was too long, Paul said, "I'm glad to see you." Then, "You look pretty. I mean nice. I mean both."

"I'm glad to see you, too. We missed seeing each other at Christmas," Connie said. *Oh, he is pretty, not cute or handsome, but pretty.* "We need milk, but our jug is still at the house. I can bring it tomorrow."

"Don't worry about it, Connie. I can come get it after supper, if that's all right."

After supper, I like 'after supper,' "That's too far to walk for an empty milk jug," Connie said.

"No, no. It's okay. I can drive my daddy's truck."

"Okay," Connie said with a growing smile. "I'll see you after supper."

Paul pulled a jug from the icy water of the cooler. "I'll take it out to the car." He closed the distance between them and followed her to the car.

He spoke to Elizabeth and put the jug in the floor board. "I'll see you after supper."

"Thanks," Connie said as she extended her hand to Paul through the open window. She didn't offer a shake, she only let her fingers slide across Paul's open palm as the car moved away.

Paul looked at his hand. "Damn," he said and walked into the milk room.

Elizabeth looked at her little sister, "So, Paul is coming calling after supper tonight?"

"Oh, no," Connie answered quickly. "He is coming to get our empty." *But maybe he is coming to call.*

"I see."

Thanks to Clara, the house was neat and clean. Supper was early and only a sandwich. Connie cleared the table and washed the few dishes and went to her room. When she came down, she had changed into her new jeans with the cuffs rolled up, bobby socks, loafers, and a sleeveless shell.

Elizabeth smiled.

"I'm going to the front room to watch for Paul."

Remembering her waits for Bill, "You can see better from the front bedroom upstairs. I rinsed out the jug. It is on the kitchen table."

"Okay."

"It is cool enough this evening you could entertain your caller on the front porch. I'm going to be in the parlor."

Connie thought about protesting her sister's characterization of Paul's visit, but decided it was all right. She headed upstairs.

Ten minutes later, Connie ran down the stairs and called out, "He's here."

Elizabeth waited until the truck stopped. She walked into the front room and stood beside the window. She could tell Paul had on a clean shirt. *Pretty well dressed for an empty milk jug.*

On the porch, Connie said, "Paul, I will go and get the milk jug in a minute, but first I want to ask you something."

Seeing Connie in jeans at first relaxed and relieved Paul. *That's the Connie I know.* When he was two steps from the porch, Connie turned, and he watched her. *No, this is not the Connie I know, this is a real girl, a pretty girl.* He felt the swelling start. *Damn, I need to sit down, or this boner will be pointing like a bird dog.* He said, "Take your time, Connie. I want to talk to you too," Paul sat in the swing with his hands covering his lap. "What did you want to ask me?"

Connie didn't have a question, she knew she wanted to spend some time with Paul, and a question seemed like a way to start. She stopped at the door and turned to him, "I haven't been to school in Greensboro for a long time, and I don't remember many kids I was in school with. I thought this summer, I might try to find some. Do you know Julie Ware or Beverly Moore?"

"Bev's still in here, but I think Julie's family moved. Who else?"

"I can't think of anyone else right now. What did you want to ask me?" She walked to the swing and sat beside Paul.

Paul was as much at a loss for a conversation starter as Connie had been, but he tried, "What's your school like in Columbia?"

"I guess it's big compared to Greensboro High. We had two homerooms in every grade."

"Is it called Columbia High School?" Paul continued.

"Oh, no. It is University High School. But there is a Columbia High, and Dreher, and a new one out in the country and one in the mill village. We played them all in basketball."

"University High?"

"Yes, we are across the street from the University of South Carolina. Some of our teachers go there. They are studying to be real teachers. That's like when I was at Barrow in Athens."

The school talk was the start. Soon the conversations across the creek and at the dairy let them become friends again. They had been on the porch swing for nearly an hour and had not touched even though they were only two inches apart. They had not looked at each other at the same time. Even so, Paul felt a twinge every time he stole a glimpse of the new Connie. And when Connie looked at Paul, she couldn't push away the image of him taking a bath that hot afternoon.

"It's getting late," Paul said, "I need to go." He shifted on the swing to get his feet on the porch floor. As he moved, the screw holding the chain pulled from the ceiling, and his end of the swing hit the floor with a loud thump. Paul rolled out flat on his back.

Connie tried to catch herself but didn't and fell face to face toward Paul. He instinctively put his hands out and succeeded in breaking her fall by catching a breast in each hand. For an instant, he realized his good fortune. Connie's knee found his crotch. Quickly, he released his treasures and threw his arms to the sides with a loud "uh". Connie settled squarely on top of him with an explosion of air from her lungs.

The few seconds they lay there seemed much longer as each tried to make sense of what happened.

"Paul, are you okay?"

"Yeah, I think. I lost my breath. How about you?"

"I'm okay," she replied, "My leg is caught on the swing and my knee hurts where it hit something hard, the floor, I guess."

"Yeah, the floor," Paul mumbled.

"I don't know which way to move."

"Hold on and let me see about your leg," Paul said as he brought his arms together behind her back. He couldn't resist a little squeeze that pulled her closer. He released his hands and slid his right hand down her back, over her hip and down her leg to her knee where her lower leg went up to the swing. "I can't reach where you're caught, but I see how. When I move the swing, move your leg," Paul said. He caught the end of the swing and pushed it, and Connie's cuff came loose.

Now they were lying together, face to face, with Paul on his back and Connie on top straddling his leg. Paul had both hands together behind her. Connie raised her head. Neither spoke, and both closed their eyes. They closed the short distance between their lips.

"What's the matter? I heard a noise," Elizabeth said as she opened the front door. "Oh! Are you hurt?" she asked as she saw Paul and Connie on the floor and the swing hanging from only one chain.

"No," Connie said aloud and "darn" under her breath.

Paul, now eyes wide open, looked at Connie and questioned, "huh?" Rolling to his side, he said, "No ma'am, Mrs. Brown. We are okay. The swing sort of dumped us on the floor when the chain came loose.

Paul and Connie stood and brushed themselves off. "Mrs. Brown, I'll come tomorrow and fix the swing. I think all I have to do is put in the screw that holds the chain in the ceiling."

Elizabeth said, "We won't worry about the swing now. I'm glad you are both okay. Connie, it is getting late."

"I need to go. I have to help with milking in the morning."

Elizabeth said, "See you later," as she went into the house.

Connie grabbed Paul's hand and said, "Come tomorrow, and I will help you fix the swing." Still holding his hand, Connie followed Paul. "Bye," she said, as he started the truck.

Remembering, Paul extended his hand from the window and let his fingers slide over her open palm as he moved away. "I will see you tomorrow."

When Connie reached the porch, Elizabeth came to the door with the empty milk jug, "He forgot this."

Connie took the jug from her sister and said, "He did, didn't he? I'm going to bed now."

In his room, Paul relived those few seconds on the porch floor a hundred times. *She wanted to kiss, I know she did. God, she felt good. She likes me.*

Connie lay in her bed too. *He touched me. Maybe it was an accident, but it felt good. He hugged me; he really did. I know that wasn't an accident. He rubbed my back, my butt and down my leg. We would have kissed if Elizabeth hadn't come out.*

Connie had not had visions since she spent the night with baby Aaron, but lying in her bed, she saw Paul down to his shorts getting ready to bathe in the creek. She walked to him, and as she walked, she took off her shirt. In his arms, they kissed. She saw herself step back and reach behind to unhook her bra. The vision stopped there, but it replayed as a dream during the night, never going further than when she reached back.

After dinner, Paul drove in his dad's truck. He had a step ladder and climbed to look at the place where the screw had come out.

"I see a problem," he said. "I need to get the brace and bit from the shop. I'll only be a minute."

"I'll go with you," Connie said and was in the truck before he got to it.

When they returned, Paul climbed the ladder and made some measurements with his dad's folding rule. "It is hot here near the ceiling and sweat keeps getting in my eyes," he said as he climbed down. He took a blue bandanna from his pocket and folded it into a triangle. "Would you tie this behind my head?"

Paul knelt and Connie stood close behind him. His blond hair was damp and matted at the neck and temples. Drops of sweat ran down his back. She leaned forward and placed the big end of the bandanna on his forehead and breathed in the smells of him. Not bad smells, but not girl smells. Last night's vision filled her mind. She pushed it back and tied the bandanna.

"Thanks. That helps, but I'm still going to take off my shirt."

Connie swallowed.

Paul unhooked one strap of his overalls from the bib and pushed the other down over his arm. He grabbed the neck of his shirt from behind with his thumb and pulled it over his head. As he wiped his face with the shirt, the bib fell forward and his overalls slipped down, catching on his hips. An inch of his boxer shorts showed, and his chest and back glistened with sweat. He looked like he did when he stood in the creek, except now Connie was right beside him. She reached out.

As he moved the shirt from his face, Connie caught herself and said, "I'll take that."

"No, it's a mess," Paul answered, and he shook the shirt out and hung it over the banister. "It will dry quick." He slipped the straps to his overalls on and climbed the ladder again. "That's much better."

As Connie looked at his nearly naked back. *Not better, but not bad.*

"Whoever put the swing up put the eye screws through the ceiling and not into a joist. I have them in a joist now. It won't fall again," Paul said as he folded the step ladder. "Could I get some water?"

Embarrassed she hadn't thought about it before, Connie asked, "Would you rather have tea?"

"Water is fine, but if you have some ice, that would be great."

Connie came to the porch with a pitcher of ice water and

two glasses as Paul loaded the ladder and his tools in the truck. "Let's test the swing while you drink," she said.

He took the glass from Connie and drank it all at once. "Just what I needed." He poured himself a second glass and sat beside Connie on the swing. He gave a little push, the chain squeaked against the screws. "See, it won't fall now."

"Thanks," Connie said and slid a little closer to him.

"Connie, I like being close to you, but I'm dirty and sweaty now. You ought to be careful."

"I'll be careful," she said and moved closer.

Without looking at her, Paul said, "They have a dance at the VFW over at Siloam this Saturday. If Daddy will let me have the truck, would you like to go? I'll get you home as early as Elizabeth says."

Her heart skipped, "Yes, I would like to go. Elizabeth is my sister, not my momma. We can stay as late as we want." Connie knew the last part wouldn't hold up.

"I think Daddy will let me have the truck, but I may have to be home at eleven. Now, I have to go help with the milking, or Daddy won't let me have anything." Paul handed Connie his glass as he stood, "I'll talk to you tomorrow about Saturday." Paul never bothered with the steps and was in the truck heading down the drive before the swing stopped moving.

I have a date! I have a date with pretty Paul Hall to go to a dance! Connie opened the door to the house and called, "Betty May, Betty May, I can't dance."

21

Paul and Connie got to the VFW early. They could hear the band, but didn't see many people. "Brother told me to park near the way out, so we don't get boxed in," Paul said as he turned the truck close to the driveway. Connie was out and looking before he could open the door for her.

"Come on, Paul, I want to see."

Hand in hand, they walked toward the music. The band played on a low platform under a big tin roof supported by telephone poles. Under the peak of the roof, a faded metal sign announced, "VFW Pavilion." A woven wire fence needing attention surrounded the pavilion. A low cement block building was off to their left. Two men sat at a table by the gate. A small sign read "Admission 25 cent." Paul gave the first man two quarters, and the second man said to Connie, "Hold out your hand."

Reluctantly she did, and the man pushed a rubber stamp down on it. When he lifted the stamp, she saw a black "V".

Connie looked at the mark and then at the man. "Little one, if you and blondie there go out to your car for a little private time, that's so you can get in without having to pay again." He stamped Paul's hand.

The band started *Orange Blossom Special*. The dark-haired boy stepped out front and leaned on his fiddle and the notes seemed to fly from it. The other four in the group backed him until the banjo picker took a turn.

Paul said to the guy next to him, "They are pretty good; they got a name?"

"Not that I heard," he answered. "They are from somewhere in Carolina. Yeah, they play pretty good, but we ain't heard them sing anything. The girl playing the guitar is supposed to be a good singer and can sing *Tennessee Waltz* just like Patti Paige."

"I want to hear that," Paul answered. "You want a Coke, Connie?"

"Not now. Let's get a seat and listen."

After a few more tunes, the banjo player said they were going to take a short break.

Paul swung around so he faced Connie. "I know this is a dance, and I asked you, but I can't dance a lick, not slow or fast. Mamma tried to show me some steps, but it didn't take. I want to dance with you, and I will try, but don't expect much."

Connie took Paul's hand, "I can't dance either. Elizabeth says you don't have to do much in a slow dance but hold on and move your feet a little. We can try."

"I'd like to."

The band started coming back to the stage. It was getting dark and the crowd had grown. The fiddle player was out first, and three girls came to the stage and talked to him. He smiled but didn't say much. When the whole group was on stage, the banjo player announced, "This is a tune you hear every day on the radio. Listen to our base player." They brought everyone to their feet with *Chattanooga Shoe Shine Boy*.

The next song was a slow ballad, and another followed. When it started, Paul and Connie went to a corner of the dance floor. Mostly they held on to each other, and that was enough. They did move their feet.

Rock Around the Clock was next, and Paul and Connie didn't try, but the tune seemed to please most of the crowd. After a few more tunes, the fiddler announced, "We are going to take another break, but first here's another popular tune."

Connie recognized the song immediately as something she had heard in Columbia. She was surprised to hear a colored singer's song in Siloam. But she liked *Too Young* and pulled Paul to the floor again. "This is going to be our song," she said.

When they walked off the floor, Connie said, "I have to go to the bathroom."

The line for the ladies' room came out of the building, and Connie fell in place. Two older girls stepped in behind her. Paul said, "I will meet you by the light pole over there."

"He your boyfriend?" the dark-haired girl behind Connie asked.

Connie answered, "I guess."

"You better be sure. There are some girls here from Lincoln County who'd eat a pretty one like him right up."

"Leave her be, Julie," said the other. "He'll be fine, but he is cute."

Julie said, "Sorry, doll. You're pretty cute too. You can hang on to him." Turning, "Shirley, I know I've been kinda bitchy, but I'm late."

"Late! How late?"

"More than two weeks."

"Shit," said Shirley. "That's long. You ever been that late before? Does Bubba know?"

"No to both," Julie answered. "And Bubba ain't gonna find out. We broke up for a while. Tonight, is the first time we've been out in two months."

"Who, Julie?"

"Oh, some fellow I ran into at a place near Athens. He said he had girl troubles. I said I had boy troubles. We had a few beers. One thing led to another," Julie answered.

"You were careful, weren't you?"

"No, we were drunk."

"What are you going to do?"

"Right now, I want to pee. Later, Bubba is going to have a really good night. You know, just in case."

Shirley said, "I've heard of a woman in Augusta."

"Yeah, everybody has heard of somebody somewhere, but I'm not going to think about that now."

Both Shirley and Julie had accepted Connie as a silent member of their conversation. Julie looked at Connie and said, "Good looking as he is, you mind what you do. You are too damn young to be worrying about what's on my mind, but you are not too young for it to happen."

Connie smiled and nodded in agreement. The line had moved inside so Connie was next to the door. It opened and two girls came out.

Shirley said, "It's a two-holer. Julie, you go first."

When Connie and Julie came out, Connie started walking toward the light pole and Paul.

Julie called, "Wait a minute. I meant what I said about staying out of trouble. For now, be happy with a little grab what you can in the back seat of his daddy's Buick. Where are you from?"

Connie stopped and turned, "Greensboro," she said, "But most of the year, we live in Columbia."

"Well, Greensboro-Columbia…"

"My name is Connie."

"Connie, I don't want my troubles to be all over the county. So, don't say anything."

"I won't," Connie said as Shirley joined them.

Connie stepped closer to Julie and touched her belly.

At first Julie recoiled, then she moved forward to Connie's touch. She closed her eyes and smiled.

With her hand flat against Julie, Connie said, "It is a girl, a beautiful little girl with red hair like my sister's."

Shirley looked at the unlikely scene before her. "You know for sure, don't you?" she said more than asked.

Never taking her eyes from Julie, Connie answered, "Yes. Yes, I do."

Julie sighed and Shirley took her hand. They walked toward the pavilion.

Connie paused and called, "Julie, you have to tell him; you have to tell Woody."

Shirley stopped, dropped Julie's hand and looked at Connie. Julie kept walking. In a second Shirley screamed, "Woody? Woody!"

A red-haired boy came running past Connie, "Shirley," he called, "what's the matter?"

Connie felt a knot in her stomach, and she stopped. *Woody. Why did I know? Why did I say his name?*

Connie walked a few steps with her head down. When she neared the light pole, she looked and saw Paul. Two girls, they looked older, were talking to him. Paul was looking at the ground.

Lincoln County girls. Connie walked between them and Paul. She took his hand, "Sweetheart, let's go." Connie never slowed and Paul had to hurry.

The band had returned, and the girl who played the guitar was singing *Tennessee Waltz.* Connie stopped and looked at Paul, "I'm ready to go."

"Go home? It is early. We don't have to go now, but if you are not having a good time, I'll take you home."

"I don't want to go home. I want to go someplace where we can be alone and talk. Some things happened I need to think about."

"I don't think there is any place open."

"Let's ride then."

Connie sat by the door with her head down and her hands in her lap. Neither spoke for several minutes. At a stop sign she slid close to Paul and said, "I like you a lot."

Paul shifted to third gear, and put his arm around Connie's shoulder, "I like you a lot, too." He paused, "I thought you were mad at me, or didn't like the dance."

"I did like the dance and I'm not mad. There are other things right now. In the line, I talked to a girl who was going to have a baby, and the daddy is her best friend's boyfriend."

"A girl told you all that?"

"Some, but I figured out some, too. And, I told who the daddy is and I shouldn't have. It is going to be hard for all of them."

"Wouldn't they have figured out about the daddy without you?"

"Yes, I guess, but what I said hurt both of them tonight. I didn't like making them feel bad.

"I'm sorry, but you didn't know. Where do you want to go?"

"We don't need a place, we can be in the truck." *It's not a Buick and there's no back seat, but it will do.*

"I can go to the pasture below your house and drive to the bend in the creek. It is pretty there, and we will be close to home. It is sorta our place."

"Yes, go there. And Paul, I know what you are thinking about."

"Everybody says you can do that, tell what somebody's thinking. It's scary."

"I used to be able to tell a lot about people, and even had visions. But ever since I stayed all night with baby Aaron, I haven't been able to. It's like I used all my gift all at one time. But it seems to be coming back a little."

"You said you knew what I'm thinking about. What is it?"

"You are wondering if we are going to kiss."

"Damn."

"Don't swear, but we are going to kiss, and a lot."

Paul sped up. "It is like dancing. I want to, but I really don't know how. And, kissing is something I can't ask Momma."

Connie laughed, "I don't know either. While we ride, I will tell you some things girls at school said. Remember, we did okay dancing."

22

JULY 1951 — COLUMBIA, SC

Elizabeth and Connie found it hard to sleep every time they came back to Columbia from their house in the country. There were too many city sounds. It didn't help their apartment was on a block paved with bricks. From College Street to Greene Street, Henderson Street was red bricks. As tires hit each brick, they made a sound like someone pulling on a long zipper. It was easy to tell uphill because the zips got closer together as the car went faster. After a few days, those sounds became part of life. Connie took a little longer to get used to the train crossing by Claussen's Bakery. It wasn't loud, but the rumble seemed to last forever.

"I like our apartment," Connie said. "I like being upstairs where I can sit on the porch and read or watch what's happening. And, I like our address, 814½ Henderson Street. I tell my friends we have half of a house, the top half,"

"I like it too, Connie. I can walk to work, and you can walk to school. Some weeks, we don't drive at all."

"Last year, Mary, from downstairs, walked with me to school, but this year she walks with older kids and her boyfriend. I don't mind, I always walk with somebody."

Elizabeth taught a class for the second session of summer school, and she was gone every day until noon. Connie could do whatever she wanted, but there wasn't anything to do. She missed Paul.

After she and Paul left the dance in Siloam and parked by the creek, they figured out kissing and a little more. They managed to see each other nearly every day after that. Paul would drive over after milking, and they would sit in the swing he fixed. They went to the picture show twice. The momma of a girl in Paul's class gave her a prom party for her birthday. All the boys got little cards with five numbered lines, and they asked girls for a prom-enade and put their name on the card. A promenade was a walk around the block. If a boy had a girlfriend, he could only ask her for two. Connie didn't know the boys she walked with, but two were nice and one was silly. They knew she was Paul's girlfriend, and didn't try anything. Trying something was sort of the reason for the walks. Paul said one girl tried to get him to kiss her, but he didn't. Paul and Connie took advantage of their walks.

"Betty May, I met a new girl yesterday. She's going to be in tenth grade too."

"Where does she live?"

"Around the corner toward Five Points."

"Why don't you invite her to come visit?"

"I did. But she has to take care of her little brother and two sisters, twins."

"That seems a lot of responsibility."

"It is, and it's hard because she has to keep them quiet so her daddy can sleep. He works all night at the mill; her mom-ma works at the mill during the day. She is afraid she won't be able to go to school when it starts. Her daddy says ninth grade is enough school for a girl."

"Her daddy is like a lot of men. Even some of my professors don't think I should be studying for a doctorate."

"Phyllis, that's her name, is sad about school. I told her I would pray for her. She liked that."

"Connie, you seem to pray more now."

"I know, Betty May. I want to now. Sometimes I feel and see things about people like I used to. But it is not like when Momma was alive. I don't feel good things for Phyllis."

"Maybe we should try going to a church. The people downstairs go to the Methodist church uptown. We could try it."

"Let's do, Betty May."

After church, they walked past Columbia High School and around the corner to Caldwell's Cafeteria. They both liked sliding their tray along the shiny rails, looking at the food. It all looked good. It was hard to decide, and you could pick a dessert before you ate.

At their table, Connie and Elizabeth joined hands and Connie said a short, quiet blessing.

After a few bites, Elizabeth asked, "What did you think about church?"

"I liked the big colored window and the organ music. It filled the church without being too loud. But, Betty May, the people were so quiet. When the preacher said, "Bless the soldiers," and I said, "Amen," some people looked at me like I had done something wrong. The lady next to me held her finger to her mouth."

"I guess some churches are quiet."

"I think God wants to know you are paying attention. When you and Bill got married at Moses' church, everybody said amen and hallelujah all the time."

Elizabeth got quiet as she thought about her Bill half way around the world.

"I can go to church tomorrow with Phyllis, can't I?" Connie asked.

"Sure. You don't want to go to Washington Street?" Elizabeth answered. "Where is Phyllis' church and what kind of church is it?"

"I don't think it has a kind, and it is not far because they walk. And I want to go. Phyllis says people say things all the time."

"Take some money to put in the collection plate."

"Connie, it is after two o'clock. Where have you been?"

"Church was long and we walked home. Phyllis' mom asked me to eat dinner with them, but I knew you would be looking for me. I came home, but I am hungry."

"How was church? Did you enjoy it?"

"Oh, yes. It was good. The preacher said words like I used to say, but I didn't understand him. Sometimes, people would stand and shout and say those kinds of words too. Phyllis said the Holy Ghost had come on them."

"Did they have an organ?"

"No, they had a piano and two boys with guitars and one

more played drums. When they played, everyone clapped and moved. What do we have to eat?"

"I ate leftovers from last night. There's some left and they're still warm."

"That's all I want. Brother Best, he's the preacher, said I could come anytime I wanted."

"Do you want to go back?"

"Yes. The people were all friendly and talked to each other. I used to have the Holy Ghost come on me sometimes, didn't I?"

"I guess."

"I can go there again, can't I?"

"Sure. Maybe I will go with you. Is that okay?"

"I would like that, Betty May."

AUGUST 1951 — GREENSBORO, GA.

"Here comes Paul," Connie shouted from upstairs. When she ran through the parlor she continued, "It's too hot to sit on the porch. I might get him to drive down to the creek."

"Connie," Elizabeth said. "You two have been together every day since we came home, but you haven't really gone anywhere. Why don't you go to the picture show?"

Connie paused long enough to explain, "We can't talk in the picture show. We've only been here a little over a week, and we have to go to Columbia on Sunday, and there's not a holiday until Thanksgiving!"

"You best be careful. Remember what Momma used to tell me."

"What's that?"

"Beware of an unguarded moment."

Connie stopped and looked at her sister as she considered what she had said. "Betty May, I think I love Paul. No, I do love Paul, and I want to marry him."

"That's fine. Paul would be a good husband. But you are only fourteen, and now is not the time to be thinking about marriage, or the things married people do. We've talked about that."

As Connie went down the hall to the front door she called, "I know, Betty May, I know. Don't worry."

"Even though I'm going to the same school, it feels different to know I'm in the tenth grade," Connie said. "How much longer until we get to Columbia, I'm getting hungry."

"Not much. We are nearly to Lexington. I packed some sandwiches. It doesn't seem like it, but it is Sunday, and there won't be places open to get supper," Elizabeth answered.

Connie was quiet for a moment. "I need to decide what to wear the first day of school. It will be hot, but I don't want to wear a summer dress."

"You do sound like a real sophomore."

"Phyllis' daddy let her come to school. They got a colored lady to take care of the little children," Connie said. "She is going to be my best friend this year."

Routine settled in. September was hot and October started that way.

"There's a letter from Bill!" Connie shouted as she came up the stairs.

Elizabeth ran to meet her and took the letter. "He mailed this two weeks ago," she said. "I wonder why it takes so long...?" and her voice trailed off. "He's coming home! He's coming home!"

"When?"

"Thanksgiving, the Saturday before and for two weeks. Two weeks! He wants to know whether to come here or Greensboro."

"Greensboro, Betty May, please let's go to Greensboro for Thanksgiving. We haven't been there since school started. I can miss those three days of school."

"Yes! We'll go to Greensboro. In fact, we'll go the Saturday before Thanksgiving. I have one class to teach on the Tuesday before, and I'll give them a free cut. Yes, Connie, we'll spend Thanksgiving as a family in Greensboro. I have to write tonight."

Connie walked in from church, "Betty May, Brother Best says we are going to have a big revival meeting at the fairgrounds. He picked me and Phyllis to be altar girls."

"When is this going to happen?"

"It is going to be the first three nights in November. You can come. Our church is going to get a bus to drive out to the fairgrounds every night. They'll have a big tent. It is for people all over town, not just our church."

"Who is the preacher, Connie?"

"I don't know, but Brother Best says he is really good."

Phyllis caught Connie at the Horseshoe. "Daddy said, they started putting up the tent this morning. Some of the singers will be here today and practice. He might go out this afternoon and help. Do you want to go?"

"I can't go today, maybe tomorrow. How will you get back?"

"Brother Best will be there and I'm sure some others from church will be there."

Walking to school on Wednesday morning Phyllis was excited. "This is going to be fun, Connie. The tent is beautiful. There is a stage. a big altar and a high pulpit for the preacher. A quartet was practicing, and they were good. I can't wait."

"Are you going out today?"

"No, Daddy has to go in to the mill early because he is going to be off on Thursday and Friday. But the best thing is we are going to have Communion with the preacher."

"What do you mean?" asked Connie.

"The preacher gives one altar girl or boy Communion before each service. You are to go Thursday, I'm going on Friday, and a boy from another church is going on Saturday. Girls get special gowns too, and we can keep them."

"How am I going to get there early?"

"Brother Best said to tell you he would take you in the first bus."

The tent was in the field behind The Steel Building on Rosewood Drive. When the bus pulled in, they were greeted by a man in a black suit with a red and white bow tie. "Brother Best, welcome," he said. "I think with this weather we will have a good crowd tonight." He turned to the few others on the early bus and said, "Go find a seat in the tent. There are bathrooms in the building there," and he pointed to The Steel Building.

Except for Connie and Brother Best, the others started for the tent or the building.

"Is this tonight's special altar girl?" the man asked.

"Yes, Johnny," Brother Best replied. "This is Cornelia Du-Bose. We think she is very special."

"Pleased to meet you, Miss Cornelia. You can call me Johnny," he said as he extended his hand. "Come with me and you can get ready."

They walked across the grounds to where there were some little trailers and tents. Johnny stopped at a small silver trailer parked apart from the others and said, "This is the pastor's private chapel. Please go in."

At one end was a picture of Jesus like the one in her mother's session room at home. Under the picture, there was a table with a cross, goblet, and bread. The table sat on a low platform the width of the trailer. The floor and the platform were covered with a thick burgundy carpet that extended up the windowless walls. Small lights like candles in sconces provided the only light except what came through the open door.

23

As Johnny stepped through the door behind her, he asked, "How tall are you?"

"Five feet, four inches."

He pushed a curtain on the wall aside and ran his hand along gowns hanging from a rod. "Ah," he said. "This looks right."

"That's beautiful," Connie said.

"It's for you. For Communion, and for you to keep. I'm sure it will fit nicely. I am leaving now. Undress completely and put this on. Here is a bag for your clothes and undergarments. When you are done, sit here and wait until the pastor knocks."

Connie nodded.

"If you are ready, tell him to come in and stand to greet him, then kneel at the table. He won't be long, and congratulations for being chosen," Johnny said as he stepped from the trailer and closed the door.

Connie looked closely at the gown. It was beautiful and quite modest. The silk taffeta first layer had a high, round neckline and long sleeves. The body was covered from the shoulders to the floor with a fine white lace. White tulle with white satin ribbon bindings covered everything.

For a minute she was concerned about undressing in front of Jesus, but decided it was okay. *This is so pretty, and the silk feels so good against my skin. I could wear this for Paul on our wedding night.* She packed her clothes in the bag and sat.

Johnny stood at the closed door a moment and started toward the big tent. The pastor watched from the shadow of the nearest trailer. When Johnny was half-way, he stopped and lit a cigarette. At the flash of the match the pastor walked to the trailer. He knocked and called, "Cornelia, may I come in? Are you ready?"

Through the door, he heard, "Yes, sir. Come in."

Closing the door behind him, "Cornelia, I am Pastor Samples, Albert Samples."

"Pleased to meet you, sir," she said, and turned and knelt at the table. She looked up, "Momma?" she asked quietly.

Samples ignored her and continued, "You look lovely this evening. Perfect in fact." *Yes, just fucking perfect.*

Connie started to stand, but Samples put his hand on her shoulder as he knelt. He moved his hand to break a piece of bread and put it in her mouth. He passed the goblet to her and said, "Take, drink. The blood of Christ shed for you. Drink it all."

Her mother screamed, "Run Connie, run!" and Connie jumped for the door and was out. She ran so fast everything was a blur until she saw a house. It was her house, her door with 814½ on it. She reached for the knob. A sharp pain in her belly stopped her short. She looked again and the numbers melted away in drops of blood.

Connie knew she wasn't home. Even before her eyes opened, she knew. She knew too what he had done. With her eyes open, she stared at one spot on the ceiling trying to make it come into focus. She could hear his breathing. *I'm going to sit.* Connie pushed herself up and felt another quick, sharp pain. The gown which had been around her neck fell to her waist. There was a spot of red growing on her thigh. She tugged the gown down and pressed it into the red.

"Oh, you've ruined your gown for the service. No matter, I'll get you another," Samples said. "I think you enjoyed our time together. It was our special Communion. I'm glad you wanted to share with me."

Connie closed her legs tightly on the gown.

Samples turned toward Connie. "I know how special you feel, but you shouldn't tell anyone. This was for us. Besides my child, no one would listen to you. And you would get in trouble for telling things that aren't true. Now, let me get you another gown, and we'll go to the service together."

In the dim light, Samples looked directly at Connie.

Connie met his gaze and quietly said, "Momma, I need you." The bulbs on the sconces seemed to be brighter. For the first time since she had taken the fever from baby Aaron, she knew she had her gift. In the light, she looked into Albert Samples' soul. The images from his past rushed before her like she watched from an express train as it sped through a depot.

Samples saw them too,...*he stood beside her bed and heard the voice of Lillian Gish Poovey. Rage filled him, and he grabbed the brass lamp on the bedside table and crashed it into the sleeping Lavinia's face as hard as he could.* He cried out "Tuttle."...*he took the pink crayon from the box on the art table... the back of Roscoe's head lined up with the end of the barrel of his daddy's .22 rifle.*

"No! Stop!" he screamed. "What are you doing to me?" Nothing stopped....*Deborah, naked, turned in the bed as he opened his knife.* Samples knew he couldn't stop. He ran from the trailer.

Connie knew he would come back. She took off the gown, and wiped away more blood, and put on her dress, shoes, coat, grabbed the bag with her underwear, and ran into the darkness beyond the trailers.

"Cornelia, Cornelia," Johnny called as he looked for her.

Connie crawled under a big truck parked by the fence.

As he walked by, she saw the outline of his legs against the glow of the big tent. "Cornelia, we need to help you." He moved away but kept calling.

When she heard music coming from the big tent and didn't hear Johnny anymore, she slipped from under the truck. Staying close to the fence, she found a place to crawl under and cross to the railroad track. She turned onto Rosewood Drive and kept walking. An hour later, she opened the door to 814½.

"Connie?" Elizabeth called. "I didn't expect you this soon. Is anything the matter?"

"Not really. I didn't feel well and decided to walk home."

"That's not a good walk at night. Are you sure you are all right? You don't look like you feel well, and you are a mess."

"I'm okay, but I'm going to take a bath and go to bed."

There was no more blood and the pain had eased, but as hard as she scrubbed, she couldn't wash the feeling away. In her bed, she prayed with plain words, then she cried. Sometime in the morning she slept. In her dreams, she saw again the images from Albert Samples mind. There was more detail, but she didn't understand or know what she was seeing.

"Do you feel better this morning? It is time for school," Elizabeth said from her door.

Connie turned over to her and rubbed her face. "I feel better, but I'm not going to school this morning."

"You never miss school. Do I need to take you to the doctor?"

"Oh no! No, I don't need to go to a doctor. Let me rest today. I'll be fine."

When Elizabeth left for her classes, Connie bathed again. Sitting in the tub, she remembered Phyllis was to be the altar girl tonight. *I have to warn her.*

At quarter to three, Connie left the apartment and walked to the end of the Horseshoe across from University High School. She saw Phyllis.

"Where did you go last night? I thought you were going to bring in the cross. Are you sick? You didn't come to school today," Phyllis said as she walked to Connie.

"I'm not sick, but something bad, really bad happened last night. You can't go tonight."

"What are you talking about? I have to go tonight. I'm the altar girl. Daddy will make me go."

"Sit over here so I can tell you," Connie said as she walked to a bench beside the sun dial. "Albert Samples is an evil man."

"The preacher?"

"Yes, He, he, he did…," Connie cried into her hands.

"What, Connie? What did he do?"

Connie looked at Phyllis, "He must have put something in the communion wine that put me to sleep for a few minutes. When I woke up, my gown was all under my neck and I was naked, I hurt and there was blood. He did it to me while I was asleep."

"You mean he…," Phyllis searched for the word.

"Yes, and, he will do it to you if you go."

"That's against the law. You have to tell the police."

"He says it was my fault that I wanted him to do it. The police would believe him. He's a preacher. They wouldn't listen to me," Connie answered.

"Did you want him to?"

"No, no!" Connie wailed. "He hurt me and I bled, and, and you don't even believe me."

Phyllis moved to the bench beside the sobbing Connie and put her arm around her shoulders. "Connie, I believe you, I do. Daddy will make me go. It's the first thing he's been happy about in a long time. You have to tell somebody. Elizabeth?"

"I can't, not now, she might not believe me either."

"I'm scared. What can I do?"

"Phyllis, the man who took me to his trailer asked if it was my time of the month. When I said no, he told me if it was, I couldn't be an altar girl. You tell him you are having your period."

"What if that doesn't work?"

"If that doesn't work, you have to run."

"Boss, the girl for tonight is, uh, ritually unclean. We don't have another girl. Do you want a boy?"

"No. You don't have time to get one of the stinky little shits bathed. Goddamnit! The girl last night was a strange one. She knew what happened right away, but she might be scared enough not to make any trouble."

"I couldn't find her last night. Preacher Best asked me why she didn't come in with you. I told him she got scared. He didn't say nothing to that, so she ain't talked to him. And, the cops ain't been around."

"Good. Columbia is driving me fucking crazy. I hope to hell this show is making some money."

"We're doing okay. Today is pay day at the mill. If we can get some of the hands in before they spend it all on liquor, we can have a good week. Remember it is pay day when you take the offering."

"I will. Grace ain't free at this church. Where are we taking this show after this? I'm ready for a break."

"After next week, we don't have anything until the two-day gig before Thanksgiving."

"Good. Where are we next week?"

"Georgetown County. A little church out toward Andrews wants to pray against the big whorehouse in Georgetown."

"They can pray in one hand, and shit in the other. They'll see which one fills up first. The Lodge ain't going nowhere. But it is sinful, and I'm agin' sin, so we'll take 'em the show. Get us a couple of girls to say they worked there, and we will save them. Saving whores is always a good thing. That's a high dollar cat house so they'll have to look pretty good. Get me a boy tomorrow, at least they don't bleed."

24

"What did you tell your daddy about not carrying in the cross last night," asked Connie.

"I told him the same thing I told the man," Phyllis answered.

"What did your daddy say about that?"

"Nothing. He don't like that kind of talk. He walked away. He won't say nothing else about it, ever. Connie, did I do right?"

"Yes, he would have done the same thing to you he did to me. He's done other bad things, real bad, and lots of them."

"What do you mean, Connie?"

"It's hard to explain, Phyllis, but sometimes I see things. I know he's done a lot of bad things. I cry every time I think about what he's done, and what he took from me and Paul."

"Paul! You and Paul?"

"I wanted the first time to be with Paul and he took that away from me." Connie put her head in the crook of her arm resting on the chair and sobbed.

"You still haven't told your sister?"

"No, and I'm not. Phyllis, please don't tell anybody."

"I won't, but what about Paul. Will you tell him?"

"I don't know. I don't know what to do about any of this. For now, this all has to be my secret."

"Connie, we will leave early tomorrow, about six o'clock. Bill is supposed to get to Atlanta about noon, but he doesn't know when he will get to Greensboro."

There was only a pink glow to the sky behind them as they crossed the Congaree River into West Columbia. By the time they crossed the Savannah River, the sun lit a crisp fall morning. Elizabeth looked to her sister, "You sure have been quiet this morning, really for the last few weeks. Is there something wrong? Maybe between you and Paul?"

"Nothing's wrong, I have a lot of things to think about. Me and Paul are okay."

"I know you want to see him as much as I want to see Bill."

"Uh-huh."

"Wait, Betty May, wait a minute."

"I have to wait, the light is red." They were stopped at Greensboro's only traffic light. "What are you looking at?" Elizabeth asked as Connie stared out the window. Over her shoulder, Elizabeth could see a poster. She read aloud the printed part, "Revival and Tent Meeting, Good Preaching, Good Singing, Pastor Albert Samples," and hand lettered at the bottom, "November 20 and 21, Fairgrounds. Colored Section."

"Drive, Betty May! Go right now."

"I can't the light's still red. Isn't Albert Samples the preacher that was in Columbia?"

"I don't know…Yes…Drive!"

The light changed and Elizabeth started out Broad Street. "Ever since the night you walked home, I've known something has been wrong. You need to tell me."

Connie didn't answer until they reached Godfrey's Store Road. "I can't tell you, Betty May, I can't."

"I can't help unless I know what's wrong."

"Nobody can help. It's already done."

"Someone can always help." And, a moment later, "I see Paul walking into the dairy. Do you want to stop and tell him you're home?"

"No, please don't stop."

At the house, Connie jumped from the car and ran in by the never locked back door. Elizabeth took her suitcase and walked upstairs to her room. Connie had not gone to her room or the bathroom. Going down the front stairs, Elizabeth heard quiet crying from the front room. She walked in.

Connie was kneeling before the St. Paul altar piece, and she held her mother's cross in both hands. "Betty May, Momma wants me to tell everything."

"Thank goodness. Let's sit in the parlor."

"Not now. I want Bill and Paul to be here. Momma said so. She said Bill will know what to do."

"Okay, but it might be late this afternoon. What about Paul? When could he come?"

"Paul will come when I say—tonight, after supper. I'll go tell Paul now."

"I guess after supper will have to do. See, you do seem better deciding to tell us."

"I do, Betty May, but it is bad and sad and evil. Momma said I had to be with people who love me." Connie stood and embraced her sister. "I love you, Betty May."

"I love you too. Now, I need to see Clara. I'll drive you down to the dairy. I suspect Paul will bring you back."

"I'll get out here and walk to the dairy." *I don't know what to say to him now. After supper I can tell all, Momma will help me. But now, I want to see him up close. I want to touch him, and I want him to hold me. He might not want me after tonight.* She pulled the door open, "Paul."

Paul looked and smiled. "Boy, I've missed you."

All of Connie's thoughts stopped, and she ran to him, threw her arms around his neck and started kissing wherever her lips landed. Their lips soon found each others. Connie stood down from her toes and let her arms fall to Paul's waist.

"Wow," Paul said, "I guess you missed me too."

"Yes, so much. It's been two months." She wrapped her arms around him and lay her head on his chest.

Paul held her close and moved his hands to the small of her back. "Two months is too long," he said.

Connie pushed away, "No, Paul, don't. I have something important to tell you."

"Okay."

"Not now, Come to the house after supper? I want to tell you, Betty May, and Bill at the same time."

"Sure, I'll be there. I didn't know Bill was coming home."

"He's on leave for two weeks. I'm going now."

"Wait a minute and I will take you."

"No, I want to walk." She gave Paul a quick kiss on his cheek.

When Connie walked into the kitchen, Elizabeth said, "I have bad news. Clara says Mr. Moses is very sick. Dr. Parker says it is cancer, and he doesn't have long."

Connie clenched her fists and closed her eyes tightly. "Momma didn't tell me about Mr. Moses, and I didn't know. This is hard Betty May, maybe too hard."

"We will go and see him soon."

Bill's brother-in-law picked him up at the airport in Atlanta and drove him to Lithonia. He was in uniform and only two cars passed his thumb before he got a ride in a truck heading for Augusta. He got out at Jim O'Neal's station in Greensboro.

"Take your old truck while you're here," Jim said.

From the front bedroom, Elizabeth saw Bill's old pickup coming from town. It turned at their lane. When Bill got out, she ran to him. It had been nearly a year since she had seen her husband.

Connie stood out of sight at the front door while they kissed. They stood with their arms wrapped around each other without speaking. Connie stepped onto the porch and let the door bang close. Bill looked and called, she ran to him, kissed him on the cheek and joined the embrace. She took his bag and led them into the house.

After a few minutes in the parlor, Bill said, "I've had a long day, and I would like to clean up and get out of this uniform. I might take a nap."

"I could use a little rest, too. Connie, do you want to take a nap?"

"No, I'm going to the front room and talk to Momma."

Before Bill could ask, Elizabeth said, "Connie has something to tell us. Something has been bothering her. Paul is coming after supper so we can all hear what she has to say."

Paul arrived and they all went to the parlor. Connie sat in her mother's chair in the corner. "I need to say a prayer," she said, and knelt on the ottoman. Unusual for Connie, she prayed silently.

Still on the floor, Connie started, "Something bad, no, something terrible, happened to me." She looked at Paul, "and to us." Her story started with meeting Phyllis and going to her church. She told about the revival and how excited she and Phyllis were to be chosen to be altar girls. She didn't look at anyone when she told what happened in the trailer.

Elizabeth cried out and moved to her sister. Kneeling beside her, she wrapped her arms around Connie's shoulders.

Paul jumped up with his fists clenched.

"He hurt me, and I bled. He said I wanted him to do it. I didn't. I was asleep. I didn't know what was happening. All I remember was drinking the wine. Please don't hate me. I didn't want it to happen."

Paul came to her. He dropped to his knees and took her hands. His voice cracked in anger, "Who was this?"

Connie wept as one with a completely broken heart. Between sobs, Connie called, "Momma."

Releasing Paul's hands, she rubbed her eyes and regained some composure. "There's more, much more, I have to tell you."

"Go on," Bill said.

"When I woke up enough to sit, I looked right at him, and I had a vision. I saw the things he had done, to other girls, lots of them, and to boys too."

Elizabeth interrupted, "Boys?"

"Yes," she said, "and I saw people he killed, a lady and a little girl. I don't know who they were or when it happened but seeing them scared me. He knew what I saw, and it must have made him afraid. He ran out. I got dressed and got out of the trailer. I had to hide under a truck because his friend looked for me. They would have hurt me. When he quit looking, I walked home."

"Elizabeth, is this the first time you've known about this?" Bill asked.

In tears, "Yes. Oh, Connie, you never said anything. You never told me. I've been so worried about you. Why didn't you tell me?"

Elizabeth stood, "Oh, oh my God! It's him! The preacher that's coming to Greensboro next week is the one who did this to Connie."

"He's a dead man!" Paul said.

"Elizabeth, what are you talking about?" Bill asked.

Elizabeth explained about the poster they had seen when they got to town.

Paul said, "Our preacher has been talking about him coming for a month." He paused, "Maybe I'll ask him to have Communion with me."

"Connie, why didn't you tell Elizabeth?" Bill asked.

"I didn't think she would believe me. Even Phyllis didn't believe me at first."

"Phyllis, I forgot about Phyllis," Elizabeth exclaimed. "She was going to be an altar girl, too. Did he hurt her?"

"No, she finally believed me," Connie answered.

"Sheriff DeWitt will believe you, Connie. I'll call him tonight. He will stop him from hurting anymore girls," Bill said.

"I'll stop him, I'll stop him in his tracks," Paul said.

Bill looked at Paul, "I understand, Paul. I know how you feel. But let's do this right and get Sheriff DeWitt to help us. Okay?"

"For right now," Paul said.

"Connie, what about the other things you saw? The lady and the little girl, what about them?" Bill asked.

"It was all so fast, I can't tell you much. Momma helped me this afternoon. She'll help me tonight. But I think the lady and little girl were a long time ago. Oh! And the little girl's brother. He was one, too. This is hard, and he is a mean, wicked man. I hate him."

Bill hung up the telephone, "Ben will be here right after church. He will listen to you, like we have. Paul, you come back. Now let's all settle down and see if we can rest."

Bill held out his hand to Elizabeth. As she stood, she said to Connie, "You need to rest too. You will have plenty of time to talk to Paul."

"I know, Betty May, but I'm going to stay down here in the front room for a while. I need to be near Momma. Paul will go in a minute."

Connie took Paul's hand and led him to the front door as Bill and Elizabeth took the backstairs.

Paul started to speak, but Connie put her hand to his mouth. "Tomorrow," she said.

25

When Elizabeth came down, she found Connie asleep in the big chair in the front room. She started the coffee and called from the hall.

Connie opened her eyes and curled tighter in the chair. "I'm cold," she said as Elizabeth walked to the door.

"Go to your room and rest some more."

"I felt close to Momma last night, and I think I know a name."

"A name?"

"The name of the lady Pastor Samples killed."

"Are you sure?"

"No, but Momma is."

"Come here," as she opened her arms to her little sister. "You're so grown in many ways, but still a baby in so many others." Elizabeth sobbed, "Why did this happen to you?"

"I prayed a lot last night. I prayed for Paul. This is hard for him. It is hard for us. I love him. It wasn't supposed to be this way for us."

"I know. He knows it wasn't your fault."

"He does. Paul is good, really good. I wanted my first time with him, our first time."

Elizabeth didn't answer, but said, "You go and rest. I'll wake you in time to dress. Clara is coming to help with dinner."

"Good, I want to see her. Momma told me about Mr. Moses. She says he is at peace. I love Mr. Moses."

Paul got to the house first, and he and Connie sat on the swing. They held hands but didn't talk much at all. Paul looked, "Who's that coming?"

"I think that's Diane Weston's car. She works for Sheriff DeWitt."

"Good morning," Diane said. "The sheriff called this morning and said it was important. What's wrong?"

"A lot," Connie answered. "Please come in and I'll tell all about it when Sheriff DeWitt gets here."

As they opened the door, Paul looked back. "There's the sheriff's new black Ford."

All six were seated in the parlor. Clara was in and out with tea.

"Connie," Sheriff DeWitt said, "Bill told me what you said last evening. Would you go over it all for me now?"

Connie repeated her story in detail. Diane was taking notes and nearly dropped her book when Connie told what happened in the trailer. She said, "Shit." Nobody noticed.

Sheriff DeWitt asked, "You were an altar girl and that's why you went to his trailer?"

"Yes, to have Communion," Connie answered.

"And, you think he put something in the wine to make you pass out?"

"Yes, sir. And I think he did that to an altar girl or boy every night."

"And when you were passed out, he...he took advantage of you?"

"Yes, sir."

There was a loud crash followed by, "Dear Jesus, have mercy!" Clara stood in the kitchen doorway holding an empty tray. Broken glass, tea, and ice lay at her feet. "Miss Elizabeth, I'm sorry and don't mean to be paying no mind to your business, but Reverend Manigault say Angel is the altar girl and supposed to have Communion with Reverend Samples on Tuesday. What must I do?"

Everyone turned to Sheriff DeWitt.

"Don't worry about Angel," he said. "I won't let anything happen to her. That's a promise." After a moment, he asked, "What time is Angel supposed to have Communion?"

"I don't know."

Sheriff DeWitt looked at each person in the room. "I can run this man out of town, and maybe make life tough for him for a day or two, but that won't stop him or make him pay for what he did to Connie and the others." All nodded an agreement. "The only way is to catch him with Angel."

Clara cried, "Oh no."

"Let me finish, Clara. We will get him before he can hurt Angel. How old is she, and will she know about what we're talking about?"

"Angel is the same as me, fifteen," Connie said.

"Yes, sir, Sheriff DeWitt, she know," Clara said. "Young'uns grow up so quick anymore. But she ain't been with no boy. Please don't let him hurt her."

"You have my word." Turning to Bill, "My regular deputy, Buddy, is on vacation this week. I'm going to recall you to active duty for Greene County. And, Paul, I know you want to help so I'm going to deputize you."

"Yes, sir," Paul said proudly.

"We'll meet tomorrow about eleven in the morning at Moses' cabin," the sheriff continued. "Clara, can you get Jacob Manigault there?"

"Yes, sir."

"Now," standing, Ben DeWitt said, "don't say anything to anyone about this. Paul don't tell your momma or daddy. I've got some things to do now, so I'm leaving. Diane, find out if Samples filed all the paperwork right for him using the fairgrounds. He's from Carolina, right?"

"Yes, sir," Connie answered.

Elizabeth added, "Winnsboro, I think. It is a mill town, north of Columbia."

As the sheriff turned to leave, Connie said, "I haven't told you anything about my visions of the other things he did. Bad things."

"Connie, I want to know about those things, but first I want Samples in my jail." Sheriff DeWitt walked out.

"Betty May," Connie said, "last night, I dreamed about Momma. She told me he had killed people, a lady and a little girl and her brother. It was when he was a boy. Momma said somebody's name was 'Turtle', or something like that."

Diane wrote, 'like Turtle' in her book.

"Remember all you can, Connie," Diane said.

"I will, but I don't think Sheriff DeWitt believes me about what I saw in my visions."

"Sometimes Sheriff DeWitt needs a little help," Diane said. She looked at Bill, "Right?"

26

"What did you find out about Samples' paperwork?" asked Sheriff DeWitt.

"Not much we didn't know," Diane answered. "All the county paperwork is in order, and our churches paid for the permit. Manigault's church and two white churches are the sponsors. They get thirty percent of the net offering."

"I'll bet they wouldn't have gotten much, but now they won't get anything," DeWitt said. "I'm going to the fairgrounds to see how they are going to set up. After, I'll go talk to the other preachers to see when Samples is getting here."

"Will you tell them anything about Connie?"

"Not for now, I want to keep this quiet."

Diane knew she was going to make the call. She dialed zero. "Sally, this is Diane. Please get me a long-distance operator." A pause and Diane said, "Operator, this is Agent Diane Weston with the Greene County Sheriff's Department, Greensboro, Georgia. I need the police department in Winnsboro, South Carolina...Yes, I'll wait."

"We have no number for a police department in Winnsboro," the operator said. "I do have a listing for the Fairfield County

Sheriff's Department. Winnsboro is in Fairfield County. Will that do?"

"Yes, that's fine, and thank you for checking."

"Sheriff Kitt," Diane said, "we are in the middle of an investigation and have a name that may be connected to a crime, possibly a murder, in your county several years ago."

"Yes ma'am," Sheriff Kitt replied. "What is the name?"

"It might sound like 'turtle'. Does that mean anything to you?"

"Jacob, thank you for coming on short notice," Sheriff DeWitt said as he walked toward the group he had asked to meet. He extended his hand to Reverend Manigault. Surprised, Jacob took it. Before he released Jacob's hand, Ben DeWitt put his left hand on their grip and looked at Jacob. "Jacob, there is evil in our midst, and we must work together."

"Yes, sir."

Sheriff DeWitt continued, "It is Pastor Albert Samples."

"Pastor Samples? Evil? I don't understand," Jacob said.

Sheriff DeWitt explained, "We think he does this often. It seems most don't know what happened. They are all young."

"Connie thinks he does this to boys, too," Bill added.

"I believe Connie DuBose, but I can't use what she says to make a good case against him because it all happened in South Carolina. I can run him out of town, and make it hot for him in Georgia, if I can't do much else. Jacob, I want to stop him. Do you know when Samples is supposed to get here?"

"This afternoon." In a moan, "Sheriff, his man, Johnny, say Samples wants to have a private service today for the workers.

Johnny done picked out a boy from Reverend Campbell's church to take Communion and carry up the cross."

"What time?"

"Johnny told Reverend Campbell to meet him at the tent at two o'clock."

"At least we don't have to worry about Angel, but we don't have much time. Travis, Paul, you follow Reverend Manigault. The two of you can act like you are helping. Bill follow me to Little Zion Church. I'll ride in with you. They don't need to see my car on the fairgrounds again today."

Sheriff Kitt took a long time to respond to Diane's question. "Deputy, what did you say your name was?"

"I'm not a deputy, Sheriff Kitt, but I work for Sheriff Ben DeWitt in Greensboro, Georgia."

"Yes, ma'am. I don't know anyone named Turtle, but Tuttle is the name of a woman who was murdered here about twelve years ago. We never solved the case. Do you think Tuttle could be the name?

"Yes. We didn't find out about her or the murder, but the name came up in our investigation. Do you know Albert Samples?"

"The preacher?"

"Yes. Would he have been around when the Tuttle woman was killed?"

"Yes. His momma is still here. His daddy died in '49, and he came home and preached the funeral. He would have been twelve or fourteen when Miss Tuttle was murdered. Why?"

"I shouldn't say without Sheriff's DeWitt's approval, but we think he may be involved in her murder."

"Why do you think he is connected to Miss Tuttle? We had two more murders right after her, a little girl and her brother. The state boys said the same person did all three."

Diane swallowed hard, "Sheriff Kitt, we may have some information about the murder of a brother and sister. I don't think I can say anymore until I talk to Sheriff DeWitt. I think he will want to talk to you."

"And, I want to talk to him as soon as possible. Those murders have been hanging over me for a long time. If it hadn't been for the war, I would have never got re-elected. Do you think he can call this afternoon? Please let me have your telephone number?"

"The little silver trailer must be his chapel," Paul said as he, Travis, and Reverend Manigault walked across the fairgrounds. "It's where the sheriff said it would be, and I don't see another trailer like it."

"There's nobody by it. The sheriff said Johnny would stand guard," Travis said. "He's the one we have to get before he can warn Samples."

"I see him," Jacob said. "But I don't see Reverend Campbell. Good, we are early."

"Travis, you stay with Reverend Manigault," Paul said. "I'll wander over by those men, but I'll keep an eye on you."

"Good afternoon, Mr. Johnny. It looks like you've gotten a lot done," Reverend Manigault said. "Has Pastor Samples arrived?"

"Yes, he's here. He is in his chapel praying."

Reverend Manigault took Travis' elbow and squeezed. "So Reverend Campbell is already here. Where is he?"

"No, he's not here yet."

Reverend Manigault loosened his grip on Travis. "I want to tip my hat to him when he comes. Travis, see if you can help someone. We must do everything we can to spread the word."

"Yes, sir," Travis said, and he headed in Paul's direction.

Paul saw Travis coming and moved away from the men he had joined.

As Travis walked past, he said, "Samples is in the trailer. The boy's not here yet. Reverend Manigault will take off his hat when he comes."

"I'll tell the sheriff and stay where I can see the trailer. You follow Johnny and the boy when they come," Paul said.

"We can't get any closer to the trailer," the sheriff said. "It is too open. We will have time to get in when Travis and Paul get rid of the watchman. Can you see Jacob?"

"Yes, and he still has his hat on," Bill answered. "Wait a minute."

They watched as a man and a slender boy who looked to be twelve or thirteen walked toward Reverend Manigault and Johnny. Reverend Manigault removed his hat and nodded to the man and boy. Johnny and the boy started toward the trailer.

"That's him," Bill said.

"Where's Travis?" asked the sheriff.

"He's by the corner of the tent. He saw everything. He'll start this way when Johnny gets past him. Paul saw them too, and he moved to where he would be closer," Bill said.

At the trailer, Johnny knocked and opened the door. He showed the boy in and followed him, leaving the door open.

"It seems like they've been in there a long time," the sheriff said.

"Door's open and Johnny's inside, I don't think anything is happening."

Johnny came out and closed the door, moved a few feet away and lit a cigarette. Travis broke into a trot and waved his hand like he saw someone by the gate. Since Travis was not heading toward him, Johnny watched, but he didn't seem concerned. Paul moved behind the end of the chapel trailer.

Johnny walked a little further away. Paul called, "Johnny."

When he turned to see who called, Travis put on a burst of speed and quickly covered the distance to Johnny. He lowered his shoulder into the middle of Johnny's back and wrapped his arms around his waist in a perfect tackle. Paul stepped out, and as Johnny fell his face met Paul's knee with the crunch of breaking teeth and bone. There was no air in Johnny for him to call out. Paul and Travis dragged him behind the next trailer and handcuffed him to the hitch.

As soon as Johnny was down, Bill and the sheriff ran to the trailer. Bill stood with his ear to the door. He mouthed, "I don't hear anything."

Ben took his .38 from his pocket and pointed to the door knob with it. Bill reached for the knob and turned. The door was not locked. He nodded to the sheriff, pulled the door open, and followed him in.

A naked Albert Samples turned. All he saw was two large shapes in the dark trailer. "What the hell?" He called. "Johnny!"

"Put your hands up. Don't move. Johnny ain't coming," Sheriff DeWitt said.

Samples raised his hands. "Why are you in here? We were preparing for a service, we were going to have Communion. I am Pastor Albert Samples."

"Well, Pastor, I am Sheriff Ben DeWitt and you and I are going to a communion of sorts. Bill, see about the boy."

The boy was unconscious and lying on the platform. His belt was unbuckled and his zipper down, but otherwise he was dressed. "He's breathing okay, and his pulse seems normal," Bill said.

"Move over Samples," Ben said, "so I can see."

Samples took a step, and the sheriff moved toward the boy. "We'll get him to Dr. Parker as soon as we can."

For an instant Samples had a clear path. He dived through the open door, rolled and came up running, but right at Travis. He cut to his right, but it was the wrong turn, and he quickly learned the full effect of right arm trained lifting gallon jugs of milk and hay bales. Paul's fist landed squarely in the middle of Samples' chest. The blow lifted him off the ground. He landed with a dull thud. Twitching and wheezing on the ground, the naked man voided his bowels and bladder.

Sheriff DeWitt stepped from the trailer with his pistol in

hand. He looked at Paul and Travis standing over Samples and slid his .38 in his pocket. "Paul, you see it is true," he said. "you really can knock the crap out of somebody."

Travis turned away so the sheriff would not see him laughing at the white man on the ground.

By now, Reverend Manigault and others had gathered around.

"Sheriff is everything okay?" Bill called from the trailer.

"Yes, Deputies Hall and Jackson have things well in hand. How is the boy?"

"He's coming around pretty quick. I think he'll be fine."

"Keep him inside for now." Looking at the gathering, Sheriff DeWitt called to a man in the crowd, "Willard, you think you can find a bucket of water?"

The man answered, "Yes, sir. There's a hose pipe by the concession. We'll get some. Come on, Joe. Help me."

Continuing to speak, Sheriff DeWitt said, "Y'all back away a bit. This ain't no pretty sight to see. Travis, see if you can find something in the trailer to cover the prisoner's nakedness."

Travis nodded and headed to the trailer.

"Paul," the sheriff asked, "where's the lookout?"

"We handcuffed him to the trailer yonder. He had this in his hand." Paul handed the sheriff a small bottle.

Without speaking, Sheriff DeWitt read, "Chloral Hydrate," added a grunt and pocketed the bottle.

Travis returned with Sample's coat and spread it over his middle.

"That's better," the sheriff said. Looking at the growing group, Sheriff DeWitt stepped toward them and held his hands up. Silence was instantaneous. "We've had some bad things happen here today," he began, "and, it is not over. Reverend Manigault will tell you all he can about what's happened and why. For right now, I will tell you Preacher Samples, here, and his man over there are under arrest. Jacob, please take everyone to the tent and explain."

Jacob Manigault had to take a breath when the high sheriff of Greene asked him to speak for him. "Yes, sir," he said. Stepping close to the sheriff, he asked quietly, "Do I have to tell about Miss Cornelia?"

"Thank you for thinking about her, Jacob. No, don't mention her name. Say I had a confidential informant."

Reverend Manigault repeated "confidential informant," to himself. He spoke to the crowd, "Please follow me to the tent."

"Sheriff, reckon this is enough?" Willard said as he and Joe carried a wash tub half-full of water.

"That ought do," the sheriff answered. "Travis, move the coat, and you boys pour some on his front side."

As soon as the cold water hit Samples' belly he cried out, "Stop."

"Turn over, boy," the sheriff ordered, and pushed his shoulder with his foot. "On your belly and spread your legs. Hit the other side, Willard."

Samples moaned again. "You want some more water, sheriff?" Joe asked.

Bill Brown watched a minute from the trailer door, ducked inside. When he came out, he was holding a wool Army blanket. "Wrap him in this," he called to Paul.

"No, we don't need any more water, and the blanket will

work. Let's get these two locked up. Travis, put these handcuffs on Samples," the sheriff ordered.

"Yes, sir."

"Put his hands behind his back."

Travis repeated, "Yes, sir." The few still watching saw something that had never happened before in Greene County, a colored man putting handcuffs on a white man.

"Bill, you and Paul take the other guy out to the camp. Tell Monroe to lock him in the isolation cell."

27

"I don't know what I can put on Albert Samples, but he is about as bad as they come. I'm going to stay here tonight and watch him. Maybe the attention will make him sweat. In the morning, I'll want you to take notes when I question him. It won't be pretty."

"After what he did to Connie, I can handle it. But, Sheriff DeWitt, sir, I need to tell you what I've found out."

"Sheriff DeWitt, sir? That sounds like Agent Weston talking."

"Yes, sir."

"What have you been up to?"

"You remember Connie said there were other bad things he had done?"

"Yes, but we can't use any of that against him."

"I know, but Agent Weston called Winnsboro, SC and talked to Sheriff Lewis Kitt." He wants to talk to you as soon as possible."

"How would Connie know anything about what he'd done? Hell, how would her mother know? I can't tell another sheriff a fifteen-year-old girl's dead mother told her Samples was a killer." Sheriff DeWitt sat for a long moment, "Maybe I can have a confidential informant."

"Pardon?"

"Never mind, see if Agent Weston can get Sheriff Kitt."

"Sally, I need the long-distance operator again." A few minutes later, "Sheriff Kitt, can you hold a moment for Sheriff DeWitt?"

As he took the telephone, he covered the mouth piece. "Thanks, now you go home, but stop by and tell Gwen that I'll be here all night with our prisoner, and to bring supper for both of us. Lock the door."

Diane nodded.

"Sheriff Kitt, this is Ben DeWitt."

It was after six when he hung up. "Damn," he said as he looked at the two pages of notes he scrawled during the conversation. He walked to the bathroom past the cell. Samples stood. When he returned, he said, "Boy, you're in a mess of trouble. If you've got any real connection with the Lord, you ought be using it."

"I want a lawyer."

"The Lord will likely do you more good, but you'll get one soon enough."

"I want a lawyer now!"

When the sheriff heard a key in the front door, he left Samples. "Diane, you didn't have to come back. Gwen would have brought this."

"I know, and she didn't have to feed me some of your supper. It was an easy trade for me. She says for you to be careful. Did you find out anything from Sheriff Kitt?"

"Quite a bit. He says SLED, that's their GBI, has finger

prints from the Tuttle woman's house and a matching one from the young girl's murder. If he can get the fingerprint guy from SLED, they'll be here tomorrow. It's time for you to go home. I'm going to eat and make some calls."

Warden Frank Copelan's truck was parked behind the jail when Diane arrived for work. The game warden stood as Diane entered the office.

"Frank is going to mind the prisoner for a little while this morning. I'm going to question Samples' side man. After a night out there, he might be in the mood to talk."

"Good morning, Frank," Diane said as she sat. "Has our prisoner had breakfast?"

"Yeah," Frank answered, "I brought him hot bologna, eggs and gravy from Geer's. He didn't seem interested."

"Gwen's cooking last night spoiled him," Diane answered.

Sheriff DeWitt said, "Call me as soon as you hear from Kitt, but I don't want Samples to know anything about him. I'm going to the house and clean up."

"Are you going to question Samples this morning?" Diane asked.

"No. With what I found out from Kitt, and them coming, I'll wait until they get here."

Diane hung up the phone as Sheriff DeWitt entered the jail. "That was Kitt," she said. "He and the fingerprint guy are fixing to leave Columbia. They ought to be here by two."

"What did you find out from the other fellow?" the warden asked.

"He's only been with Samples for about a year, so he claims he doesn't know anything about any murders. But he had plenty to say about Samples and his 'show'—that's what Samples calls his services."

"What about Connie and the boy yesterday?"

"He arranges Samples' private Communions with the young altar girls and a few boys, usually one before each show. He uses knock-out drops. Most don't realize what happened until later, if ever. Samples paid a few parents off."

"What a rotten son of a bitch. Can you make a case? Would he testify against Samples?"

"Just for assault, we got there before he could do anything else. Maybe there's something in South Carolina, but Johnny wouldn't make much of a witness."

Frank stood, "Tell you what, get him on assaulting that boy and send him out to Monroe. Once those fellows at the camp find out what he's in for...he'll get what he deserves. Sorry, Diane."

The phone rang, "Bill wants to talk to you,"

Sheriff DeWitt hung up, "Connie wants to come see Samples."

"Talk to him? I don't think that's a good idea," Diane replied.

"No, she wants to look at him, to see what's in his mind. Her Momma told her she had to, so she could tell me all he'd done."

"She can't tell you anything that can be used in court, can she?"

"You're right, but she might tell me something I can use

when I question him, or something Sheriff Kitt can use. If Samples recognizes her from Columbia, he might get rattled."

"I would have thought she would be scared of him."

"According to Bill, she's obeying her mother. How the hell did I get in the middle of this, Agent Weston?"

"Connie, you don't need to worry about him. He is handcuffed to the door and has leg shackles. All he knows is someone is coming to identify him. Ready?"

Sheriff DeWitt stood beside Connie holding her hand. "Look at us, and keep your eyes open."

Columbia! That's the little bitch from the first night in Columbia. I knew she was going to be trouble when she ran, and we couldn't find her. Why did I run? I should have killed her. Samples smiled and looked directly at Connie, "Hello, my dear. I'm sorry you ran away and didn't get to bring the cross in. But we had a very nice Communion."

"Look at her and be quiet." the Sheriff barked. He felt Connie's grip grow tighter, and her hand become warm.

She did not take her eyes from Albert's. At first, she felt like she was again on the express train rushing by the scenes of Samples' past, but the train slowed, and one by one, she could see the things he had done.

Just like in his trailer in Columbia, Albert couldn't stop remembering each one: Lavinia Tuttle, Lillian Gish Poovey, Roscoe Poovey, Deborah, Miss Dixie and the Australian girl who didn't wake up from the drops. Again, and again they played through his mind, and each time Connie saw more.

How do I stop her? Albert pulled tightly against the bars of the cell door. He said, "Little darling, when I'm out of here, we'll get together and do some more of the things you liked. We'll have fun."

"Go out, Connie," the sheriff said. As soon as she turned, De-Witt brought his night stick down on Samples' forehead. Blood spurted and ran down his nose. He collapsed to his knees with his hands still cuffed to the door. "Later, maybe you and me will have a little fun."

In the office, Connie fell into Elizabeth's arms and sobbed.

"Diane, call Dr. Parker. The fool may need a stitch or two. Connie, are you okay?"

"Yes, sir." Connie answered. "He killed them all."

"The lady and the brother and sister?" Diane asked.

"Yes, and three more. Two ladies close to where he lived and one girl far away. He gave her too much medicine."

"Connie, are you sure you don't need to rest a little?" Sheriff DeWitt asked.

"No, Momma wants me to tell what he did."

For the next forty-five minutes, Connie described the six murders. She did not let anyone interrupt for a question, and when she finished telling about the girl from Australia, she said, "Betty May, I need to go home."

"Yes, go home," the sheriff said.

"Thank you for letting me come. I've told you all he showed me. I can't talk about this anymore. Bill, please hurry."

Holding the pages she had written, Diane asked, "Sheriff, what can we do with this? It's not evidence, is it?"

"I'll be damned if I know right now. He is a mean son of a bitch. I'm not going to let go of him easy."

"You say you've got a prisoner who tried to bust out of the cell with his head?" Dr. Parker asked as he walked in.

"It's not bad, Doc, but come on and look. Diane, type what Connie said. We'll go over it before they come from South Carolina."

The black Ford with the white front door rolled past the office window. Sheriff DeWitt walked to the door and opened it. *It's a '51, same as mine, but with police lights.* "Fairfield County Sheriff" was painted on the front door. Sheriff DeWitt smiled as the passenger got out. He stepped off the porch and greeted the man, "Pete, by golly, it is good to see you. I never figured you'd come."

With hands still clasped, Pete said, "When Lewis said he needed to go to Greene County, there was no chance I wouldn't come with him." Turning to the driver, "Lewis, this is my old friend Ben DeWitt. Before the war, he once chased a load of moonshine from here to McCormick County."

"Yeah, the boy was sorry he crossed the river with that whiskey. Y'all come in and we'll talk."

The three men settled around Ben's desk. Diane continued with her typing.

Pete said, "I have the prints taken when the Tuttle woman and the two children were killed. Because of where we found them, we are sure they are the killer's. They are from a small person, so they could be from a twelve-year old, or even a woman."

Ben looked at Sheriff Kitt, "That makes sense for when Samples lived in your town, right?"

"Yes, he would have been fourteen. I never remember him being a big person," Kitt answered.

"If you've got his prints, I'll start examining them."

"Pete, I'm not real good at taking prints, so I haven't taken his yet. How about you do it?" Ben asked.

"That's no problem. I'll get my kit."

"Pete, Lewis, for right now, I don't want Samples to know you are from South Carolina. After you take his prints, I'm going to tell you something you won't believe, but I do. But I'll be damned if I know why I do."

Pete worked for the better part of an hour. He used a jeweler's loupe and a big magnifying glass. He'd go from the freshly inked prints from Samples fingers to ones taped to cards in the big case he brought. From time to time, he'd add a grunt or an 'uh uh' as he made marks on drawings of hands and fingers. Pete came to the door stretching, "Fellows, come on back."

Pete began, "I can put Samples at each murder scene. His prints were all over the Tuttle house. As for the little girl, I found a print on the..."

Interrupting, Ben said, "Pete, before you say anything else, listen to me. Diane, let me have what you've typed." He described in detail the murder of Lavinia Tuttle, as told by Connie a few hours before.

Lewis Kitt sat open mouthed. "How the hell do you know that? Even if you had my reports, there's things you said that were never in a report."

"Now, I'll tell you about the little girl, Lillian." He described the rock and how the killer had run to her and struck her in the back of her head with it. "Pete was about to say he found his print on a pink crayon that had been inserted into the little girl's vagina. Right, Pete?"

Lewis Kitt stood.

Pete simply said, "Yep."

Kitt walked back and forth the two steps between his chair and the door. His eyes went from Sheriff DeWitt, to Pete, to Diane and to the door to the hall that led to Samples' cell.

"Sit down, Lewis," Ben said. "I'll tell you about the boy. Then I'll tell you how I know this, and fellows, that part will be really hard to take."

When he finished, Pete looked at Lewis, and turned to Ben, "We can't use anything she told you in court. She can't even testify."

"Pete's right, sheriff," Lewis answered, "What can I do with what you've told us?"

Ben replied, "Samples doesn't know where this came from, so he won't know it can't be used in court, the fingerprints can. He's smart and mean, but if we work him slow, hard and long, I believe he'll break."

"Right now, I guess he's worried about the assault charges.

When we hit him with all this, he may simply fall apart," Pete added.

"Lewis," Sheriff DeWitt said, "Do you know anything about the murder of two women in a town close by? One ran a little comfort house and the other was one of her girls. Both had their throats cut."

"Oh, yes, but that was three or four years after Tuttle and the Poovey children. We've got prints, but we never solved that one either."

"Samples, too, on the night before he went into the Army. You want me to tell you how it happened?"

"Why not?" Lewis replied throwing up his hands, "You know more about what's happened in Fairfield County than I do."

"Lewis, I don't even know what it is I'm telling you. It is Connie's story, but I believe her." Sheriff DeWitt recounted Connie's version of the murders in Ridgeway.

"Damn, Ben," Lewis said, "Her story matches with everything we found at the scene, even the yellow wig. We did find a bloody heel print."

"I'll go and print Samples' feet," Pete said as he stood.

"Pete," Sheriff DeWitt said, "Let's wait until we question him about those murders. Printing his heel then might really shake him."

"Makes sense," Pete replied.

"Diane, you go on home. If we break him, you can decipher my scratching in the morning."

"I will but call me if you need me. Go ahead and finish this. Connie and those other children have had enough of this bastard." Diane added, "Pardon me."

"No need to ask, Diane. He's that and a lot more," Sheriff Kitt answered.

"If I don't see you in the morning, it was good to meet you Sheriff Kitt," Diane nodded. "And you, too, Mr. Strom. Sheriff, the beds upstairs are made and clean."

As Diane walked out the front door, Sheriff DeWitt opened the door to the back. "Albert Samples, me and you got a lot to talk about tonight."

It was three o'clock Wednesday morning when the three law men walked into the office from Samples' cell. "Ben, you were dead right. When I told him I was going to make a print of his heel, he knew we had him," Pete said.

"Six murders, that's a bunch of guilt to carry. Once he started talking, he couldn't stop," Kitt added.

"He's a psychopath," Pete said, "and as bad as I've seen. He wasn't confessing as much as bragging."

"Tomorrow, hell later today, I'll get in touch with the judge in Crawfordville and see what we need to do to get him to South Carolina. Meantime, Lewis, you and Pete go upstairs and get some sleep. I'll stay down here and watch Samples."

Sheriff DeWitt rolled his big chair to the door where he could see Samples in his cell, and the two South Carolina lawmen headed upstairs. Samples lay in his cot without moving.

28

The out of state police car parked in front of the jail already had Carey's interest.

"Carey, I can't tell you much for the paper right now. Preacher Albert Samples is in custody. He was arrested Monday on assault charges in Greene County. Yesterday, we linked him to more serious crimes in South Carolina. After questioning by me and South Carolina police, he confessed."

"That ain't much, Ben," Carey replied. "The people need to know more. They want to know about the arrest, like why a colored boy handcuffed the preacher."

"The young man was Travis Jackson. He was my temporary deputy, and he acted under my direct orders. Reverend Manigault made a statement for me. You might put in your story that Paul Hall and former deputy Bill Brown were temporary deputies too."

"Still some folks ain't gonna like that, even if it was your orders."

"I know, but they might feel different when the whole story comes out. Those folks helped stopped something as bad as I've ever seen."

"What's next?"

"Judge Morrow is coming this morning for a hearing, but Samples won't get bail. We'll hold him out at the camp until next week when the boys from South Carolina get their warrants."

"It ain't much to sell papers on. Anybody can go to the court room and hear the charges."

"Come by the house after supper and we'll talk. You might print an extra after our conversation. Meantime, why don't you talk to the preachers who put this little revival together. See what you can find out about Samples. You know anybody at a newspaper in Columbia? Samples had a big thing there the first of the month."

Since he couldn't go to press, Carey carried the news of the hearing and Ben's plans for Samples to Geer's Cafe. By noon everyone in town knew of the confession. They wanted more.

Orren Hall got the news early at the dairy with a load of sweet feed. The driver talked while Paul and Tommy unloaded the truck. As soon as he could, Paul ran to the house and told his mother. Tommy had to wait until dinner to tell.

"Momma, I'm going to tell Connie," Paul said.

"Paul, wait a minute. If you want, I would like to ask them to eat Thanksgiving dinner with us."

"I would like that, Momma. I'll ask. See you later."

Paul gave the news from town.

Connie said, "Momma told me he would tell. I don't want to talk about him now."

When Paul invited them to Thanksgiving dinner, Elizabeth looked at Connie to let her know it was her decision.

"Yes, Paul, we will come. I want to be with all the people I love right now."

"Ask your momma what I should bring?" Elizabeth said.

"Momma's been cooking all week, and Aunt Sister is coming with food too. I don't think we need anything else."

"Tell her, I'll bring some peach cobbler. What time?"

Paul wanted to say dinner time, but decided on, "I'll ask for sure and tell you later today."

"Momma said to come about noon, and we would eat at one," Paul said. It was nearly dark and too cool to sit on the porch.

"Paul, I need to help Betty May tonight. We'll have some time tomorrow and, on the weekend," Connie said as she walked Paul to the door.

When Bill turned to the Hall's house there were cars and pickup trucks parked along the lane and in the yard.

"That's a lot of cars," Connie said. "I don't see Paul's truck or the car his mother drives."

"Something must be wrong," Elizabeth said. "This many people only come when somebody dies."

"Nobody died, everything is okay," Bill said. "This is a regular family Thanksgiving in Georgia. Looks like my Mi-maw's before the war, except no wagons." Pausing, he added, "I don't guess you've ever been to anything like this. Up until your Momma died, your Thanksgivings were in a fancy New York restaurant. And since, a quiet dinner."

"Is this all family?" Elizabeth asked.

"Paul has three sisters and two brothers. They are all married and have children. He's the youngest," Connie said.

"Throw in the aunts and uncles and a litter or two of cousins, and you'd break thirty easy," Bill said.

"I can't go in with one little peach cobbler. It won't be enough."

"Don't worry about 'enough'. There will be plenty of food and desserts. Worry about remembering names, and who goes with who." Looking at Connie, he added, "Besides, this bunch may be family one day."

Bill was right on every point. Once inside, Elizabeth was absorbed into the kitchen, and Bill migrated outside with the other men. Paul was with them. Connie knew not to encroach.

Paul's mother, Beverly, said, "Connie, come with me. This is Katie and Julie, Uncle Mike's and Aunt Martha's girls. They are looking after the little children. Would you help them?"

"Yes'm."

"This is Connie. She's our neighbor, and she wants to help."

Katie said, "You are Paul's girlfriend, aren't you?"

Connie smiled and said, "Yes."

"And he helped catch the man who hurt you," Katie continued. "My daddy said he was a hero."

Before Connie could answer, one of the two babies lying on a pallet on the floor started to fuss. "Jimmy, I don't know what's the matter," Julie said as she picked up the child. "You've been fed and changed, you ought to go to sleep."

Connie sat crossed legged on the pallet. "Let me hold him."

Resting Jimmy's head on her left arm, Connie patted his tummy. He burped, smiled at Connie, and closed his eyes.

"Well, you've got the touch with a baby," Julie said.

Everyone stood at their place, and Orren said a blessing. It wasn't long. Bill and Elizabeth were at the big table in the dining room. Connie and Paul were at the third table, the cousins' table. The table didn't matter, there was too much food. At the end, the leftover food was all brought to the dining room table and covered with a big piece of cheese cloth. "That's supper," Beverly said pointing at the table, "if anybody can ever eat again."

Bill stood beside Elizabeth with one hand on her shoulder, rubbing his belly with the other. "My love, Thanksgiving was like this at my Mi-maw's. Can you get used to it?"

Orren called across the room, "Paul, it is time for us to go milk."

Sitting with Connie in the front room he answered, "Yes sir," and stood.

"Can you come later? We are going to Sandy Springs tomorrow to see Bill's mother. We may not get home until late."

"I'll be there," he answered.

Soon after Paul arrived, Elizabeth took Bill upstairs and left the two of them alone in the parlor sitting on the small sofa.

As soon as Paul heard their steps on the back stairs, he wrapped his arms around Connie and kissed her. When their lips separated, Connie buried her head at his neck and held him as close as she could. "Paul, I love you so."

She lifted her head and kissed him.

Paul's hands moved down to her waist. Connie dropped her hand to the outside of Paul's thigh and pulled him closer. She laid her head on his chest. "Tell me what happened on Monday," she said.

"Don't you know?"

"I've heard parts, but I want you to tell me. I want to know what you did."

Paul recounted the story of Monday, and how he knocked out the naked preacher.

"He didn't hurt the boy, did he?"

"No."

"Thank you for catching him."

"Connie, what were the other things he did? I've heard all sorts of things."

"I told Sheriff DeWitt, I wasn't ever going to talk about what I saw again, but I need to tell you."

Paul had tears in his eyes when she finished.

"Six people, he murdered six people, a little girl and her brother. He would have killed you." At this realization, Paul could not hold back the sobs. "I'm glad he's in jail, but I wish I would have killed him."

"No, Paul. You did the right things. You and Travis are heroes. You are my hero." She kissed him, "I'll see you on Saturday. We will have time for us."

29

"Where's Daddy?" Travis asked as he and his five-year-old, Annie, entered his daddy's cabin.

"He's out to the shed looking for something," his mother said. "Annie, you gonna help me set our Thanksgiving table? Travis, put your food there."

"Yes'm, Granny."

"Daddy must be feeling better today. I'm going to get the last of what Clara cooked."

"He had a good night. Hurry back. I want you to see about him if he's not in here in a minute."

"Daddy, what you plundering for out here? We 'bout ready to eat."

"I'm coming. I'm fixing something for later," Moses answered. "Let's go eat. I'm hungry."

"Good, Daddy. I'm glad you're hungry. Eating will help get your strength back."

Under his breath, Moses mumbled, "Ain't nothing coming back. I'm soon crossing over."

"What you say, Daddy?"

"Nothing to study about, boy," Moses said as he entered the cabin. "Liza, Clara, this is a mighty good-looking Thanksgiving dinner.

"Granny and me set the table," Annie said.

"You did good, Annie, real good," Moses answered.

"Travis, go on the porch," Moses said. "Tell me about Monday."

Travis recounted the capture of Albert Samples and his part in it.

"You say you tackled the look-out man?"

"Yes, sir, and I knocked him into Paul. Paul kneed him and busted the man's teeth. He was bleeding pretty good when Paul put the handcuffs on him."

"Paul put the handcuffs on the look-out?"

"Yes, sir."

"But you didn't tackle the preacher when he came running out?"

"No, sir. I would have, but he saw me and turned, 'cept he turned to Paul, and Paul bust him in the chest as hard as he could. His fist lift the preacher off the ground and knocked all the air out of him. I felt it, hot and stank. When he hit the ground, he messed on himself."

"You put the handcuffs on the preacher?"

"Yes, sir. Sheriff DeWitt gave me his and said for me to. Some mens had poured water on him to clean him some."

"You did good, boy, I'm proud, but you gonna get some shit from some of these crackers around here. And it don't matter about what the sheriff told you to do, or how bad the preacher was. You laid hands on a white man. You understand?"

"I do, Daddy. I done heard some of it. I can take it. But I had to do it for Miss Connie after she saved Aaron. I owed her."

"Boy, we both got that debt to pay. Is he in the jail at the sheriff's office?" Moses asked.

"No, sir. They took him out to the chain gang camp Wednesday evening, Sheriff DeWitt and them two sheriffs from Carolina. They gonna keep him away from the others 'til they come and get him."

"How they gonna do that?"

"Emerson said they got a pen with a cell they use when they got to keep somebody away from the others, like when they be sick."

Moses grunted and said, "I know the place. It is on a little hill in the back. They call it isolation."

"Daddy, they say he killed six people. They gonna give him the electric chair."

"He can get off too. Them killin's were a long time ago, and he were only a boy. White, turned preacher and all, he can get off. He's got to pay for what he did to Miss Cornelia. What does he look like, the preacher?"

"He's little, Daddy, short and po', and he's got real black hair that's most as long as a girl's, oh, and a skinny black mustache."

30

"What you doing, old man?" Liza said as she saw Moses dressing by the fireplace on Saturday morning. "You need to stay in and rest."

"I got some things to do today. Fix me breakfast and pack my pail with a little dinner. Has Travis gone to Miss Elizabeth's?"

"He's gone and took Clara and the grands to Tommy's."

"Good, I'm gonna hitch my mules."

"You old fool, you old sick fool," Liza said under her breath as Moses walked to the barn.

Travis thought I was looking for something Thanksgiving morning. He's never seen this and now he never will. He uncovered a long olive-drab, canvas pouch closed by brown leather straps. He opened the straps and removed a rifle. It was a 1903 Springfield .30-06. *Sargent told me, "Corporal, being picked to be a sniper is an honor, 'specially for a colored. This is your rifle. Don't turn loose of it." I never did, and they never asked for it, even when we mustered out.*

Twice a year, Moses took the rifle from the pouch. At Christmas, he checked it for rust and wiped it down with a light coating of oil. On Independence Day, he would slip away by himself. In a cotton field, he would set a rest at the end of a row, step off 250 paces and set a watermelon on top of a fence post. At the rest, he mounted the long narrow Winchester telescope sight on the rifle and adjusted for the distance. Lying on the ground, he fired a round. The last two Independence Days, the first and only round he fired exploded the melon. At his wagon, Moses field stripped the rifle, cleaned it, and carefully packed it, the telescope sight and the remaining cartridges in the pouch.

I bought these rounds five year ago in Athens. There be ten left. Ought need but one, maybe two. A pain from his cancer squeezed his gut and he braced himself on a post. *"I ain't got time for this right now, Lord, I got debts to pay,"* He coughed, took a breath and stood.

After a moment, he walked slowly to his wagon with the rifle and lay it under his seat next to his bugle.

Moses ate breakfast slowly. "This is good. I wanted some bacon this morning after all the chicken we had Thursday. You and Clara fixed a mighty fine dinner for us, mighty fine."

Surprised to hear a spoken compliment, Liza said, "Old man, I don't know what you are doing, but you be careful. Do you want me to go with you?"

"No. I mightn't be back until late."

At the end of Godfrey's Store Road, Moses turned left on the paved road. He met a pickup truck. *Don't know that truck. I'll tip to him, so he won't think nothing.* A quarter-mile before the gate to the chain gang camp, the road crossed a small branch. *We'll get in the water and go a ways, come out on the other side. I'll let the boys drink before we move on.*

There's the place to get out. The bank's low, but it looks soft. Moses called out and popped the reins over the mules' backs. They strained pulling the wagon through the soft sand of the bank, but as soon as the steel rimmed wheels hit hard ground, they moved easily. *Iffen we stay close to the trees, they'd have to be looking hard to see us over this old field.* The overgrown field ended at a stand of old pines, Moses got down and led his team into the trees. *I ain't far from the camp, and the place where they got the preacher is on this side.*

He led his team to a small opening. He set the brake on the wagon and threw out some hay. *Now, let me find a place.*

There's the isolation. The way it sits on the little hill, the fence ain't in line with my shot, and I can see the door plain. This log will give me cover and I can set my rest on it. I make it 225 yards.

He pulled over a fallen pine limb still with needles on it for more cover, and returned to the wagon for his rifle. At the wagon, he mounted the scope and loaded the rifle and eased to his spot. There he spread an old piece of canvas on the ground and dusted it with flowers of sulfur. *Don't care if it is November and I'm damn near dead, I don't want to spend my last days scratching chiggers and ticks. Let's see what I've got.*

He brought his rifle to his eye and turned the knob. The door to the isolation cell came in sharp. *This be good.* With the rifle still resting, he leaned forward, set the distance to 225, and settled into position.

With his eye on the cell door, Moses let his mind wander: *France, 1918, Belleau Woods, hell on earth, the 369th, the Harlem Hellfighters. Shit, I never been to damn Harlem 'til we got back. But we could fight. And we could play music. The best damn band in the Army, the brass knew it too. I learned a bunch about playing the horn with those boys. Maybe the Good Lord will give me one to play, but there ain't gonna be nobody to blow Taps for me.*

A white man came from behind the cell. *What we got here?* Moses moved his eye to the scope. *I know him, he's a guard.* Moses watched as the guard went to the door and slid the eye slot open. He stood for a moment. *I don't want to shoot with a guard close.* The man lifted the bar from the door, appeared to speak. He put something on the ground a few feet from the door and disappeared behind the cell.

In a few seconds the door pushed open and a small white man with long black hair stepped into the daylight.

That's him. That's Preacher Samples. I'll wait.

Samples reached for what the guard had put on the ground. He lowered his head to his cupped hands. When he raised his head, he blew a cloud of blue-white smoke. Samples backed up to the cell door and rested his shoulders against it.

One more draw, preacher, and you'll smoke in hell.

Samples brought the cigarette to his lips. Moses held the cross-hairs steady on the center of his chest and squeezed the trigger. With the recoil, he lost his view. He steadied the rifle in its rest and found the cell door. Wet and red traced the path of Samples' body as it slid down the door. Through the scope, he watched the body on the ground. It didn't move.

Don't need no 'nother. He's gone. Moses crawled away from his spot with his rifle and ground cloth. Now with more trees be-tween him and the camp, Moses stood and listened. *I don't hear no shouting. I guess these woods covered the sound pretty good. They'll find him soon enough.* Moses unloaded and repacked his rifle in the pouch. He led his team through the woods to the edge of the field. As he climbed into his seat, he heard shouts from the camp.

When I get across the branch, I'll stay in the woods until the sher-iff comes. I don't need to meet him on the road.

Moses saw Sheriff DeWitt's black Ford and Warden Cope-lan's truck speed to the camp. "Git up," he called to his team. At the bridge he stopped and dropped the rifle in the deep water under it. He made it to the paved road without meeting anyone. Heading toward town, he met one car, and a pickup truck passed him, but he didn't recognize either driver.

When he turned on to Godfrey's Store Road, the pain hit him bad. He slumped, and he shook the reins. The mules stepped up, they knew they were headed home. By the time they got to the cabin, Moses had fallen to the bed of the wagon, and it looked empty.

Liza was to the wagon before the mules stopped. "Old man," she called, and Moses moaned.

"Praise the Lord, you ain't dead, you old fool."

"I'm gonna die in my own bed. Get Travis," Moses said.

"Momma, I got the mules put up. Where did Daddy go this morning?"

Before she could answer, Moses said, "Son, come close. Don't study about iffen I been somewheres."

"Daddy?"

"Liza, you listen too. I ain't gone nowhere today. I been right here dying in this bed. Ain't nobody seen me, so ain't nobody gonna ask about me being out. You understand?"

"Yes, sir. But…"

"Boy, it was redemption. We always got to pay our debts."

31

They got home from Sandy Springs at nearly midnight on Friday. All slept late, Connie until 10:30. When she came down to the kitchen, Bill and Elizabeth were still at the table with coffee.

"Breakfast?" Elizabeth asked.

"Coffee, first. I'll find a biscuit or something. I ate too much the last two days."

"We all did," Bill added.

"Do we have anything we have to do today?" Connie asked.

"Not much," Elizabeth replied. "We need to get ready to go to Columbia tomorrow. Bill's going with us."

"I'm going to listen to the Georgia Tech game and take a nap," Bill answered.

"How will you get to Atlanta next week?" Connie asked.

"I don't have to come to Atlanta. I can go to a base near Columbia, Shaw Field. It is only about forty miles. You and Elizabeth can drive me there on Friday."

"Are you and Paul going out?" Elizabeth asked.

"We will do something together. Maybe go to the picture show."

Bill went upstairs.

"Connie, do you want to talk about all that's happened at the jail?"

"Yes, I do, Betty May, but not right now. I have some thinking to do."

"Don't try and do it all by yourself. And, don't leave us and Paul out."

"I won't but this is hard, Betty May, real hard."

A moment later Connie closed her eyes and hugged herself against a chill. "Moses, no, no, don't," she cried out. "Momma, help me." She put her arms on the table and lay her head on them and cried.

"Connie, what happened?…Bill, come down here," Elizabeth called. "Did something happen to Moses? Did he pass?"

"What's going on?" Bill asked.

Connie raised her head, "Moses didn't die, but the preacher is dead. Somebody shot him through the heart. It was Moses."

"It couldn't have been Moses," Bill said. "When Travis came this morning, he said his daddy was still in bed. And besides Samples is locked up at the chain gang camp. Nobody except the guards can get close to him."

"Maybe,…but he is dead."

"What if he tried to escape? Would the guards shoot him?" Elizabeth asked.

"Not unless he had a gun himself. No, I don't think…"

"I told you he's dead, and Moses shot him in the heart. I'm going to talk to Momma."

The phone rang. She hung up and called to Connie, "That was

Diane. She said Albert Samples was shot and killed at the chain gang camp this morning about 11:30."

"Damn," Bill said.

"He wasn't trying to escape or anything. The sheriff is out there now."

"I told you," Connie said. "Momma told me Samples is in hell, and for me not to worry any about Moses. The Lord will judge him. Momma says be done with all of this now, and I will. I want to tell Paul. I love him. Except…"

"Except what?" Bill asked.

"I know there is something else, and Momma won't tell me."

32

"Daddy's pickup was a mess. We moved some heifers today, and I didn't have time to clean it up. Anyway, Momma's car is nicer," Paul said. "Except the heater doesn't always work. I brought a blanket."

Paul opened the passenger door, and Connie moved to the center of the seat. *It's a Buick.* "What's the movie?" Connie asked.

"It's like *South Song* or something, I don't know exactly, but it is about Uncle Remus."

"Paul, I can't go. We were watching that movie in New York when Momma got shot. No, I can't go."

"I'm sorry, I didn't know. There might be a dance in Siloam. I didn't tell Daddy we'd go that far, but we can go if you want."

"No, I want to be with you tonight and talk. Can we go to our place by the creek?"

"Sure, I would like that too, but it might be cold."

"We've got each other, and you did bring a blanket."

When Paul parked the car, Connie kissed him before he could turn from under the steering wheel. Then she moved away. "I want to tell you what I remember about the night in Columbia," she said.

"Connie…" Paul started.

"You have to know what happened."

"Okay."

"I went into the trailer with the other man. He asked me how tall I was, and he gave me a gown from the closet. He said to put it on, and I had to take off my underwear. He left and I put on the gown. It was really nice, and I thought I would save it for you, for us."

Paul reached out for Connie's hand, but she didn't take it.

"When the preacher came in, he said I looked nice, and he was glad I was chosen for the first night. I thought I heard Momma call. He held my shoulder, and I couldn't stand. He broke a piece of bread and held it at my mouth. When I had eaten it, he poured wine from the pitcher into the cup."

Connie paused, and Paul turned more toward her and started to move closer.

Connie held up her hand. "He gave me the cup and said the part about this being the blood of Christ. He said drink it all, it was real wine. I gave him the cup, and I don't remember anything until I woke up staring at the ceiling. The gown was around my neck, and he was sitting looking at me. I hurt, there was blood, and I knew what he had done. He smiled and I hated him."

"I hated him, too."

"I pushed the gown down and looked into his eyes. I could feel Momma with me and for the first time in a long time. She helped me see the evil things he had done, not clear at first, but I could see, and he knew I could. He wanted to kill me, but he ran out."

"He's dead, and you are safe with me, and I love you. It is all over. It is all over forever." Paul moved to Connie. This time she came to him.

Both in tears, they held on to each other for a long time. Connie finally said, "I hope it's over. I want to be done with him."

"You are. We are. Do you want to go home now? It is a little chilly here."

"It is chilly, but I don't' want to go home. You and me in the back seat with your blanket would be enough to keep me warm. And, I have something else to tell you; something I did."

With the blanket over their shoulders, Connie started, "Remember in the summer when I was twelve, you used to come here to get the cows?"

"Sure."

"And I'd walk on the other side and we'd talk across the creek."

"You were still a little girl, but you acted more grown-up. I think I started liking you then."

"One day, and it was hot, I saw you from the house, but you were too far ahead for me to catch you. So, I ran to this spot, on my side."

"I don't remember that."

"No, I hid, because when you got here, I saw you take off your clothes and take a bath. I was real close."

"You watched me take a bath?"

"I thought I was doing a sin, but I liked it."

Paul laughed.

"There's more. After you bathed, you did something else."

"What did I…" Paul's voiced trailed off as he remembered the usual conclusion to his creek baths.

"I didn't know about what you were doing so I asked Betty May and Bill."

"Oh my God! You told them what you saw me do?"

"Bill said it was okay, but private. Betty May said so too. The next day when Bill went to town, she told me a whole lot more."

Paul shifted in the seat.

"It wasn't right for me to watch, and I want to apologize and to ask you to forgive my trespass."

Paul relaxed and smiled, "Yes, yes, I forgive you. I don't know if Bill and Elizabeth will forgive me."

"They will, they have, but there is one more thing I have to tell you."

"What?"

"Remember when the swing broke, and I fell on top of you?"

"Yes, and I may have sinned then."

"Maybe, but if you did, I forgive you. After that, I started to have visions again. That night, I saw you standing here fixing to bathe, and you saw me. As I walked to you, I took off my shirt, and we kissed."

"I don't think visions can be sins. If they were, I'd be burning in hell right now. I have lots of visions about you."

"Let me finish. I stepped back and started to take off my bra, and that's where the vision ended."

Paul could do nothing but look at Connie.

"I want to see what happens after that, besides we deserve a really good night."

"I want to see what happens too, but it's too cold to be outside."

"It's not too cold in here. Take off your shirt," Connie said as she started unbuttoning her blouse. Paul was bare chested by the time she had her blouse off. She slipped her elbows through the straps to her slip and pulled it down to her waist. "Now kiss me, kiss me hard like I imagined."

When their lips separated, Connie unhooked her bra and dropped it over her arms to her lap. "Now."

The windows to the car were still fogged over when they got to the house. "We are going to leave early for Columbia, before you get home from church. Bill's going with us. He will go to Korea from an airbase near Columbia."

"I'll miss you. If visions are sins, I'll probably sin a lot until you come home for Christmas."

Connie laughed, "I might vision something myself. When I come back, we can forgive each other's sins."

In Friday's mail in Columbia, there was a post card from Diane saying Moses had passed on Tuesday afternoon, and the funeral would be Friday. If Connie knew, she never said. Connie asked the three of them to hold hands, and she said a prayer for Mr. Moses.

Bill drove and they were all quiet for most of the ride to Shaw Field. It was dark when Elizabeth and Connie started for Columbia.

"I hate this bridge," Elizabeth said as they crossed the Wateree River. "It's dark and hard to see, and they say there's a ghost on it."

"Don't worry about the ghost. She wants to go to Stateburg to see her dying momma. You only meet her if you are going the other way."

"I'm glad about that."

"Betty May, did Bill say he would be out of the Army this summer?"

"No, but he will leave Korea, and remember he is in the Air Force, not the Army."

"Where will he go?"

"Washington, D.C."

"Good, he can come home often."

"I will finish my degree in June, and I want to live with my husband. What would you think about living in Washington?"

"I like Columbia and my school." She was quiet for several minutes. "Would I move to Washington with you?"

"Yes, certainly. I know you would be away from Paul, but we would get to Greensboro for holidays and in the summer."

"Betty May, I have to think about this." When they passed the Veteran's Hospital on the outskirts of Columbia, Connie said, "I might like to live in Washington for a while."

"I'm surprised, but I'm glad."

Neither spoke again until they were nearly at their apartment. They had to wait for a train at Greene Street. It was long. When the last car clicked by, Connie said, "Betty May?"

"Um."

"Betty May, I'm late."

CPSIA information can be obtained
at www.ICGtesting.com
Printed in the USA
FSHW010918230919